WORKING DAYS

OTHER PERSEA ANTHOLOGIES
OF RELATED INTEREST

AMERICA STREET
A Multicultural Anthology of Stories
Edited by Anne Mazer

GOING WHERE I'M COMING FROM
Memoirs of American Youth
Edited by Anne Mazer

FIRST SIGHTINGS
Stories of American Youth
Edited by John Loughery

INTO THE WIDENING WORLD
International Coming-of-Age Stories
Edited by John Loughery

SHOW ME A HERO
Great Contemporary Stories About Sports
Edited by Jeanne Schinto

VIRTUALLY NOW
Stories of Science, Technology, and the Future
Edited by Jeanne Schinto

IMAGINING AMERICA
Stories from the Promised Land
Edited by Wesley Brown and Amy Ling

VISIONS OF AMERICA
Personal Narratives from the Promised Land
Edited by Wesley Brown and Amy Ling

WORKING DAYS

Short Stories About Teenagers at Work

Edited by Anne Mazer

PERSEA BOOKS
NEW YORK

The editor and the publisher wish to thank Harry Mazer,
who contributed the title to this volume.

For information, write to the publisher:

Persea Books, Inc.
171 Madison Avenue
New York, New York 10016

Library of Congress Cataloging-in-Publication Data

Working days : stories about teenagers at work / edited, with an introduction,
by Anne Mazer.
     p.   cm.
     Summary: Fifteen stories relate the experiences of teenagers working for many
different reasons in a variety of jobs.
     ISBN 0-89255-223-9 (hardcover : alk. paper).
     ISBN 0-89255-224-7 (pbk. : alk. paper)
     1. Children's stories, American.   2. Teenagers—Employment—Juvenile fiction.
[1. Work—Fiction.   2. Short stories.]
I. Mazer, Anne.
PZ5.W825   1997
[Fic]—dc21   *96-50243*
                                                                          CIP
                                                                           AC

Designed by REM Studio, Inc.
Typeset in Century Old Style by Keystrokes, Lenox, Massachusetts.
Printed on acid-free, recycled paper, and bound by The Haddon Craftsmen,
Scranton, Pennsylvania.
Jacket and cover printed by Jaguar Graphics, Wyandanch, New York.

FIRST EDITION

SC
WORKING

Contents

Introduction

The world is at work around us. From the moment we are born, we are part of this activity. Work gives our lives form, purpose, and meaning. It also sustains and nourishes us physically, emotionally, and spiritually. Because of work, we have food, shelter, and clothing. Work also creates books, music, athletics, and television—to name only a few of life's delights. For some of us, work can mean just a job that pays the rent, while others find a deep sense of vocation, the work we are "meant to do." We may also discover who we are (or aren't), through our work, and find our own way to contribute to society.

In this collection of fifteen, almost all original, contemporary short stories, teenagers explore the world of work and the world through work. Their situations are those teens face today. They tutor, cook in fast food restaurants, drive ice cream trucks, do chores for elderly neighbors, work in factories, clerk in hotels, and harvest crops. Their experiences can be exciting, pleasurable, and liberating, or they can be boring, painful, or harsh. Some work for pocket money, while others work for survival, or because they have no choice—work is what they've always done. Many teens work towards a goal like college, while others work out of curiosity and a desire to enter the adult world.

Work often marks a transition from childhood into maturity, and can be a rite of passage—an initiation into new responsibilities and complex relationships. For example, teenagers must deal with authority in a new way. They must make decisions and bear the consequences of their choices, such as whether to stay on a job or to quit it, or whether to obey rules or break them. And finally, work can and does bring young people into relationships with others of different ages, races, class, or culture. It can transform their views of themselves and of others.

A fourteen-year-old boy in Víctor Martínez's "The Baseball Glove" harvests chili peppers with his older brother for a day, thinking of the baseball glove he will buy. But when Immigration shows up to take away illegal immigrants working in the fields, he gains a bitter knowledge of the world, and his desire for the baseball glove takes on new meaning.

In Norman Wong's "Driver's License," Damon works at a fast food restaurant in Hawaii to earn money for a car—a symbol of freedom—but soon realizes that the job is a dead end and that the real route to freedom lies elsewhere.

Like Damon, many of the other young people in these stories use their jobs as stepping stones to college and a wider life. Lily is seventeen in Ann Hood's "Avalon Ballroom" and "already work[s] something like ten jobs" in New York City so she can get enough money to go to Princeton. In Marilyn Sachs's moving story, "Lessons," Charlotte tutors the Greek owner of a pastry shop in order to earn money to go away to college—and temporarily gains the love and acceptance she does not get at home.

In fact, many of the young people portrayed here gain far more than just money from their work. Two powerfully written stories, Roy Hoffman's "Ice Cream Man" and Kim Stafford's "Riding Up to Ruby's," depict relationships between young and old that develop in the context of work.

In "Riding Up to Ruby's," set in the rural Northwest, Rob does chores for an elderly neighbor to earn money for a bike but finds himself participating in Ruby's life in a way that forever transforms his own. Rick, a white teenager in "Ice Cream Man," drives an ice cream truck in summertime Alabama to earn money for a boat. When he meets Cap, an older black man, on his route, Cap's stories soon become far more important than the work he is doing or the boat he thought he wanted. Both Rick and Rob emerge with a deepened sense of who they are as individuals and a new idea of the work they can do in the world.

Other stories also explore issues of identity and self-knowledge. In my story, "The Pill Factory," Meredith, who comes from a middle-class family, works at a factory job that she dislikes to earn money for college. When an older woman she has trained on the glue machine suddenly quits the job, Meredith gains perspective on her own decision to stay.

Lois Metzger's "Seashell Motel" explores the sometimes humorous, sometimes scary consequences of lying to get—and keep—a job. Sixteen-year-old Cindy pretends she's nineteen in order to work in an Atlantic City hotel but soon realizes that what she has done is far more complicated than to "flip a single digit upside down."

The fourteen-year-old girl in Magdalena Gómez's opening story, "The Daydreamer," wants to work even though her parents are opposed to it. She concocts an elaborate plan to get work in a supermarket in order to earn money to go to Spain and learn to dance the flamenco. But before she can set her plan in motion, an encounter with the school principal opens up an undreamed-of work opportunity.

Viviana, the heroine of Carolina Hospital's "Catskill Snows," has a chance to sing with her stepfather's band when the lead singer gets the flu on New Year's Eve, but her mother forbids it. Choosing not to defy her mother, she realizes she will have to wait to fulfill her dream of work.

While the teenagers in "Catskill Snows" and "The Daydreamer" struggle to get permission to work, for others in these stories, work is a way of life they accept without question. In many families, children are expected to work from an early age to contribute to the family economy. "I suppose fourteen years of not knowing what, besides work, was expected from a Mexican was enough to convince me that I wouldn't pass from this earth without putting in a lot of days," says the narrator of Víctor Martínez's "The Baseball Glove." In Nora Dauenhauer's charming story, "Egg Boat," an Alaskan Tlingit family works together, and the story tells what happens when the youngest girl gets her own boat and is able to go trolling for coho salmon on her own for the first time.

David Rice's "The Crash Room" is about vocation and its sources. As a teenager, Eduardo feels the thrill of life and death working in the trauma room of a Texas hospital. When he discovers himself becoming hardened and insensitive to pain, he quits his job—until, years later, a personal tragedy helps him connect to a healer's vocation in a much deeper way.

Humor, friendship, and bad work situations unite Tracy Marx's and Graham Salisbury's very different stories. In Tracy Marx's high-spirited story, "To Walk With Kings," two best friends are forced to scrub toilets, serve food, and rake lawns when a new headmaster institutes a strict work program in their school to save money. Graham Salisbury's

"Forty Bucks" follows two teenage boys on duty late at night in a fast food restaurant, who, with the aid of an unusual customer, confront a couple of would-be robbers.

The final story, Thylias Moss's "Delivery in a Week," rewards the reader with an all-encompassing meditation on the nature of work, as the heroine grows up with a deep awareness of how work shapes her life.

Whether at home or away, most of us will spend the majority of our days at work. Through our work we sustain and create our lives, connect to other people, find out who we are, and benefit from and contribute to the world. By turns eloquent, funny, exciting, and tragic, these stories lead us to discover that work is what we do and it is how we live.

WORKING
DAYS

THE DAYDREAMER

Magdalena Gómez

*For daydreamers who
get the job done*

"I'm going to Spain," I announced to my Puerto Rican mother and Spanish gypsy father the night before my fourteenth birthday.

Looking over the top of the *Daily News,* my father, Virgilio Segarra-Fernandez, asked: "Huh?" Only one of his eardrums worked properly.

"To Spain. I'm going to Spain. I want to learn to dance like my grandmother. I want to see the castles in Valledolid. I want to go—"

"How? Your poor father doesn't even have a box to drop dead in," interrupted my mother, Lydia Segarra, as she pressed pleats into my birthday dress.

"I'm getting a job. Monday I can apply for working papers."

"No daughter of Virgilio Segarra-Fernandez is going to work. You go to school. You learn and go to college, then you can work anywhere you want," said my father, his attention going back to the *Daily News.*

"Your papí is right. And besides that, an educated woman doesn't have to get married if she doesn't want to."

Papí gave Mamí one of those serious looks of his when she said that. The air was getting thick and I thought maybe Papí's neck veins might start getting wiggly, so I just shut up.

That night, I hated my Castro Convertible bed in the living room more than ever. I would be fourteen years old in a matter of hours and didn't even have my own room. The radiator pipes played poor-people music all night long. Clink, clank, clunk, pssssst ... clunk, clink, pssst, clank; Doña Rosa's French poodle tap-danced on the linoleum upstairs, and mice held their nightly festivals inside the walls. That was it! I'd had it! I was going to school *and* getting a job, and not just any job either. I was going to be a cashier in a supermarket. I would start by packing groceries and work my way up.

I took my notebook and a flashlight into bed and wrote down everything I had to do to get ready. The first thing was to talk my father into it; next, polish my dress shoes; next, practice my cursive for the job application; next, straighten my hair with big rollers so it wouldn't look frizzy—nobody who worked in the supermarket had frizzy hair, except the cleaning guy, Don Luis, and he was really old. He had fake teeth and would put them in his mouth weird to make us kids laugh. I secretly wished he was my grandfather, since I never had one. Anyway, I filled two pages in my notebook, no skipping lines, and fell asleep like I was dead.

In the morning, my mother sang "Happy Birthday" in Spanish and told me to take a good bath, brush my teeth, and braid my hair because all the family from her side was coming for my birthday. My father didn't have a family in the Bronx. They all lived in Spain and didn't believe in taking airplanes. They were just scared of them, like my father was, but I pretended that I didn't know so that he wouldn't be embarrassed.

None of my friends from school were coming, except Amparo, because my mother thought they were all a bunch of good-for-nothings. Amparo lived with her strict grandmother and had to stay home all the time, just like me. I liked Amparo, but she was so pretty I always felt fat and ugly around her. All the boys liked her, but she had to act like she didn't care or her grandmother would have an attack of nerves. I *really* didn't care, because all I could think about was being a cashier in a pink uniform with my name embroidered on the pocket. I would do the embroidery myself. No plastic name tags for me. Sometimes you just have to be different or you feel boring.

I did all my birthday stuff, put on my dress, and waited in the kitchen for everybody to show up. The first one to arrive was Tía Consuelo. I saw the soft package under her flabby arm and I knew she had knitted me another hat with *lentejuelas* on it, those big tacky sequins. The kind of hat I wouldn't wear if my hair looked like Brillo and it was minus 100 degrees. God knows, I would never get a job wearing *that.* I thought to myself that when I did get that job, and I knew that I would, I would buy my own birthday presents, and a real fine hat made of velvet, the kind that is so soft it makes me want to cry.

A whole gang of cousins showed up, all of them too young or too old to play with. I got all kinds of presents: toys I had outgrown or clothes I'd have to grow into, but nothing that would help me get a job. One nice dress from my mother, a little too pink, good for a party, not for a job. I drank soda and ate cake, ice cream, candy—all the stuff my mom won't let me eat until I finish all my vegetables and what she calls "real food." No vegetables on my birthday; that was the best part. There was lots of real food, but with so many people to entertain, my mother didn't notice if I ate it or not.

Some neighbors showed up and told jokes that I didn't

think were funny, but I laughed anyway. I didn't want to hurt their feelings. Grownups get hurt really easily and then they get mad. So everybody laughed, played music, and had a good time. Nobody seemed to really care if I was there or not, or if I was really happy. I was just the excuse for them to have a party.

It didn't matter. All I could think about was my new job that I didn't have yet.

When I got to school on Monday, I went to the guidance counselor, Mrs. Mason, to see about working papers. Mrs. Mason said my parents would have to sign them. I told her about my supermarket idea, and she said I should try babysitting first because she didn't think I was old enough to handle money. I told her I was an "A" student in math, and she just cleared her throat and adjusted her glasses. I said, "Thank you very much" and put my working papers in my sock, since I had left my book bag in class.

I went back to class and got in trouble during Social Studies. The teacher, Mr. Moss, said I was daydreaming and that I could do that on my own time. He said daydreamers don't get into college. I told him, "Yes, you're right. They become Albert Einstein." He turned beet red and sent me to the principal's office.

Outside Mr. No-Neck's office (his real name was Mr. Nobeck) the walls were the color of *café con leche* that's a little too strong, and there was one of those "Do Your Best" kind of posters on the wall with phony smiling kids on it.

I have to admit, I was sweating. If my parents ever found out I was kicked out of class, there's no way I'd get either of them to sign my working papers, not to mention the scolding I'd get. My mother would scream and my father would give me the silent treatment, then they'd scream at each other. "She's *your* daughter," my mother would yell. My father would sit there, his neck veins getting wiggly, thinking of something to say, and once he said it, World War Three would break out, and all the neighbors would know everything I'd done wrong since the day I was born.

Mr. No-Neck came out of his office and called me in. "Miss Segarra, I hear you have a very smart mouth. Mr. Moss is very upset. His note also says you were daydreaming in class," No-Neck said, trying hard to sound like he doesn't come from the Bronx.

"I didn't mean to be smart, and I was just thinking," I mumbled, my eyes looking down at my scuffed shoes.

"Thinking? And about exactly *what* were you thinking?" he asked, poking holes in the air with his finger.

"My job. The one I'm going to get, I mean, at the supermarket; I'm going to be a cashier and save money so I can go to Spain," I said, looking at his veiny nose.

"Spain? Why Spain?" He seemed really interested.

"Because that's where my father's from. I want to see the castles and learn to dance like my grandmother." I forgot I was nervous.

"You want to dance the flamingo?"

"No, I want to dance *flamenco*. No offense, Mr. Nobeck, but flamingo is a bird."

I couldn't help myself. I was tired of people getting away with that *flamingo* thing. It's like calling Puerto Rico Porto Reek-o. I bit my lip and waited for No-Neck to blow his top.

"Well, Miss Segarra, it seems you do indeed have a smart mouth, and I'm not so sure that's such a bad thing." He said it very softly. I got sweaty-suspicious. "How do you say it, fla-mink-ko?" he asked sincerely.

"No. *Fla-men-co*," I said slowly.

"Fla-maine-co. Fla-man-co. Flamenco." He kept trying until he got it. Then he got quiet for a really long time. I got nervous again. "It's too bad you have your heart set on that

supermarket job. As he spoke, his right pointer finger was bouncing off his lips.

"How come?" I asked.

"Well, some of the seniors could use a Spanish tutor after school."

"Seniors?" I gulped.

"Yes. They need a tutor so that *they* don't go around saying *flamingo* when they mean *flamenco*. But I don't suppose you'd be interested." Nobeck looked out of his window.

"Maybe. What does the job pay?" I asked in my best business voice.

"Two dollars an hour," he said in a very flat voice, looking me dead in the eyes now.

My mind raced between Don Luis and his funny teeth and my name embroidered on the pink smock, and all the work I had done to prepare for my big interview.

"I would be happy to speak with your parents. We must have their permission," he said.

I figured he had a better chance talking my parents into it than I would, since grownups listen to each other more often than they listen to kids. "Okay, Mr. Nobeck, I'll try it." The thought of tutoring seniors made my stomach quake. "How many hours a week?" I asked, trying hard to act cool.

"An hour and a half, three times a week."

"That's only nine dollars a week." I felt limp.

"That's right."

"How many weeks?"

"Thirty. It's for the whole rest of the school year."

"That's two hundred seventy dollars." I was showing off how good my math was.

"Correct. Well?" He was standing up now.

"It's a deal."

I shook his hand. There was no turning back now. My parents had taught me that a handshake is your word of honor. They would have to sign the papers now, they would never, ever want me to go back on my word. I liked that about my parents. I didn't always like what they said, and I still hated vegetables and hats with lentejuelas, and my father's wiggly veins, and my mother's screaming, but they weren't so bad. They always kept their word. They just didn't remember how hard it was to be fourteen. Getting the rent paid was hard enough.

Nobeck said goodbye and added, "Einstein said that imagination is better than knowledge. I'm sure you'll get to Spain, Miss Segarra. And stay out of trouble. Don't stop daydreaming, just don't do it in class. And I expect you to apologize to Mr. Moss." His hands were in his pockets now.

"Yes, Mr. Nobeck. Thank you."

I left thinking about going to Puerto Rico next. Maybe I would invite Amparo. In my mind, I embroidered my name in the sky.

ICE CREAM MAN

Roy Hoffman

Now vendors use recorded jingles that play from a loud-speaker on the roof, but the summer I drove an ice cream truck you got to ring a bell. It was fastened on top of the cab and had a long cord snaking from it. While you shifted gears with your right hand and steered with your left, you'd also manage to yank that cord to set the clapper going.

I can still see children's faces appearing at the windows when the bell clanged. In Mayfair, where the homes had end-less lawns with turning sprinklers and swimming pools behind high fences, only a few kids bothered to open the door and tread barefoot down the walk, opening a pudgy hand to show me their quarters. I guess they had big deep-freezers inside stocked with treats.

In Riverbend, though, where families sat on their porches keeping cool through long Alabama summers, ice cream meant more: my bell was like the town crier calling citizens to the square. Out of their houses the kids would come, short and fat and tall and skinny and knock-kneed

and stick-limbed. They'd dig into their back pockets for
nickels, and call to their mamas for an extra dime. When
they were shy a coin, they'd beg and wheedle and plead.
Most often, I'd give in, even though Daddy warned me
about being a "soft touch."

"You're not in the give-away business," he said.

"But it's hot and some don't have enough to pay."

"I thought you wanted that skiff."

He meant Bobby Smit's boat, and how owning it meant
I'd be able to fish for bream any time I wanted. What I really
wanted was Bobby's yellow Camaro, but Daddy said sixteen
might be old enough to drive a car but not to own one.

"Yes sir," I said, "I sure do."

"That's why you've got a job, not to make a friend of
every kid in town."

I guess he didn't figure one friend I'd make wasn't a
"kid" but maybe twice as old as him.

I'd met him like a few other customers who were silver-
haired or crick-backed and called to me from porches. I'd
park the truck, hop down, and remembering what Daddy
taught me—"old people are the lucky ones"—approach
these elders with respect. In school I'd studied about the
explorers searching for the "fountain of youth," and you'd
have thought that's what I was hauling in the back of my
truck to see the bright look on their faces.

This man, in particular, was a good talker. Tall, thin,
called "Captain" by folks on his block and wearing an Atlanta
Braves baseball cap, he waited for me on the front stoop of
his shotgun house in an old porch swing whose chains
looked ready to snap. He'd wave at me to stop my truck and
hobble down to the walk.

He was part Cherokee, even though I wouldn't have
known that if he hadn't said it. My own people had traveled
from Scotland and Holland to New York before heading on to

Alabama. I had never thought about some African-Americans being part Creek or Cherokee, or even part European, until Cap told me about life in the rural county he'd come from and about how some whites, too, had the blood of a black ancestor flowing in their veins.

"We're all mixed up inside," he said.

"I don't think even my daddy knows that."

"I reckon your daddy knows plenty."

"How old are you?" I asked.

"Let's talk about ice cream."

"Well, we got chocolate-covereds, push-ups, cherry Popsicles, Dreamsicles." I took a breath, but he started in:

"See how you're working this job? Young folks now don't know nothing about workin'. When I was coming along, we didn't know nothing about playin'.

"On Saturday nights, if we had one hour to set down our load, we'd head up to the Mr. A. O. Baer's Ice and Creamery and stand out back waiting for Mr. A. O. to give us a taste. Vanilla bean, that's what I liked." He looked over the ice cream illustrations on the side of my truck, closed his eyes and licked his lips. "Tell me I can't taste it right now!"

I wrenched open the door of the truck's freezer and fished out a vanilla cup and wooden spoon, peeled back the lid, and handed it to him. I didn't even think about asking him for money.

He dug into the creamy surface, touched it to his lips, closed his eyes again and sighed.

The next day seemed made for selling ice cream and I felt my skiff getting closer. Chocolate swirls, strawberry cups, grape pops—I sold nearly a half box of each before I could head on, *ting-tinging,* to Captain's house.

He didn't trudge down to see me as before but just sat slumped in the porch swing. "Captain?" I called.

He did not move.

"*Captain?*"

"You brung me something good?" he asked, chin still down.

"Oh, yes sir," I said, relieved to hear him. "I got—"

"I been dreamin' about a big ol'"—he looked up now and grinned—"Nutty Buddy."

"Nutty Buddy it is!" I said, taking one to where he sat. As he chewed with pleasure on the rough top of the cone, he told me about how they used to make ice cream, pouring cream and sugar into a bucket, clamping a lid down on it, putting ice around the bucket sides, and sprinkling rock salt to keep the ice hard and cold.

But the secret, he explained, was in the crank.

"When I was about your age," he said, "which is old enough to think you got sense when you don't, I was workin' in Opp, Alabama, hoeing fields and toting wood. A lady named Maggie Blanchard had parties every week for her friends and hired a boy who could hardly crank her ice cream bucket, it'd come out like sweet soup. I said, 'Miss Blanchard, let me try it,' and I got that job."

He held out his arm. "Knock your fist there."

I punched him softly against his wiry forearm.

"That's steel from cranking ice cream."

I laughed.

"It's the truth!" he said testily. "Don't ever tell nobody, but I used to swipe my finger through the bucket after they'd scooped out what they wanted. You strong?"

I held out my arms and made muscles.

"What I'm supposed to be lookin' at?" He suddenly put his chin back and fell quiet. "Go on now," he whispered.

I glanced to the street. A police car had pulled up and an officer called out, "Everything all right?"

"Yes sir," I answered. "Just visiting with my friend here."

The policeman eyed me warily. I saw him study the back of my truck, jotting down notes before driving away.

"Go on now," Captain said, "git."

As I started back to my truck he added, "That first Nutty could use him a second buddy," and I pitched him another, which he caught in his big, trembling hands.

When I loaded up my truck next morning, the boss, Mr. Lewis, approached me and said, "Rick, we got a rule here which has to do with insurance. When you're working the truck you've got to stay with it. If you're fooling around helping with babies or old people, and somebody gets hurt, who's responsible? If somebody else rides the truck . . ."

"I didn't ask Captain to ride the truck!"

"On your own time, you gab all you want with who you want. But you're my employee here, and this town's full of high school kids looking for summer work."

His employee? I didn't belong to anyone and would have told him so right there except for one fear.

"Mr. Lewis?"

He was walking away but turned to me from near the ice cream storage locker where Reggie Douglas, in a hooded parka, poked his head out into the ninety-degree Alabama heat.

"Did you talk with my father about this?"

"This is your first job, isn't it, son?"

I shrugged. "More or less."

"Listen to me now. How you do at this job, or any other your whole life long, doesn't have a thing to do with father, mother, big sister, or little brother. It's about *you.*"

I avoided Captain's block that afternoon, but as I returned to the ice cream plant to park my truck, I realized that when I'd rung the bell he'd probably heard it while waiting lonesomely on his porch swing. I figured his wife was no longer living, but didn't he have children, grandchildren? Had they left him all alone with his memories of vanilla beans and bucket cranks? Cap's recollections of a life of all work and no play seemed hard to me, but ice cream sweetened them.

I took the bus back out to Springvale, to my house, and after dinner sat on the front steps listening to the crickets' nightly chorus. If I couldn't stop my truck at Captain's, what was keeping me from visiting him on my own like Mr. Lewis suggested?

Saying I wanted to go to the drugstore to look over the new month's sporting magazines, I borrowed Daddy's Impala and headed to Riverbend. It seemed different at night. Gone were the children on the front porches. As I wheeled slowly down the block to Captain's, a cluster of teenagers stood near the curb, spying me curiously as I passed. "Who are you?" their eyes said. "What do you want?"

During the day, in my job as ice cream vendor, I'd felt like I belonged; now, cruising down neighborhood blocks, I was a stranger. I was an ice cream man only for the summer, but to people who didn't know me as Rick of Robert Lee High, an ice cream man is all I was. I circled the block and drove back home.

Come morning I went to Riverbend first, clanking my bell, selling to kids who came out wiping breakfast from their mouths, happy to begin the day with a tutti frutti or blueberry pop. I didn't care if a hundred people came driving by, poking into my business; I rode to Captain's, parked, and took him a whole selection of ice creams.

He was indoors, and as I stepped inside at his invitation, I felt the air grow stuffy like I remembered from my grandparents' house when I was little. It kind of made me miss them.

On one table was a photograph of a young man in a

soldier's uniform, chest jutting out proudly, soldier's cap correct on his head.

"The day Thomas was born," Captain said, looking at the photograph, "it was so hot you could make a river with the sweat pouring off you. Mattie and me, we'd met at a church social. The pastor married us in that same church and we jumped over the broom. One year later the Lord blessed us with Thomas, named for my daddy's daddy. We'd sit right here on this sofa, the three of us, eating ice cream and listening to *Gang Busters* on the radio.

"My Mattie took cold from the bad winter of 'fifty-eight and never got to feelin' right again. The Lord took her to His home."

"I'm sorry."

"It's nothin' for sorry. I'll be goin' along soon to follow. I've kept her waitin' too long."

"Is Thomas in Vietnam?" I asked.

"Served his time and is stationed over in Berlin," he said proudly. "Married him a German girl. They came here to visit me just once, but this ain't no place for lovebirds the likes of them. Thomas said he wasn't ever comin' to Alabama again. They sat right here, the two of them, talking German, spooning up strawberry ice cream. Mattie was here too. They didn't see her, but I know she was with us. 'What's that extra dish you scooped up?' they asked. 'Who's it for?'

"'It's for your Mama,' I said. They laughed and jabbered, but I'll tell you, that extra dish of strawberry, next thing I know it was gone."

Mr. Lewis gave me a long look the next morning, but I let it pass. I hadn't seen anybody following after me at Captain's. Daddy had once told me that if a boss ever dressed you down, nod and make sure it doesn't happen again. I was too clever to get caught.

In days to come I heard more of Captain's stories about ice cream. I sat on the porch with my feet up on the railing while he tried a lemon push-up and told me about his dream of a creature made out of ice cream like Frosty was made of snow.

I was relaxing just like that when I saw another one of Mr. Lewis's ice cream trucks turn the corner and a student from Forest Prep clanging its bell. When he saw me he stopped ringing, turned his head and just drove by, rolling on out of the neighborhood.

I hopped up off the porch and continued my route. He didn't pass that way again.

Captain was adventurous in his tastes, but he could be fussy too. Once I had to traipse back to the truck to get a new item, a vanilla and chocolate bar shaped like Mickey Mouse, but he waved it off, saying, "I don't want ice cream with two eyes lookin' back at me."

He told me how once, when Thomas was ten and was burning with fever, he'd gone running to the corner for something cool and wet to bring his fever down, but that the doctor had said not to bring home anything with milk. "When I told Mr. Mirsky, the Polish man who run that store, what I was looking for, he gave me some sweet sherbet. That night Thomas's fever broke!" He paused. "You got any of that?"

Although I didn't, the next afternoon I brought him a box of rainbow sherbet striped green and pink and blue. He touched it to his lips and concluded, "I'd take this even over cold plums."

There was only a week left until the new school year and I was seventy-five dollars short of skiff money—I had given nearly that much away in profits. I had also taken to eating ice cream sandwiches, sometimes wolfing down as much as a box—five dollars' worth of ice cream—in the course of a sweltering day. That was no way, as Daddy would say, to get ahead.

I hadn't gotten much done on my summer reading list, either. I picked up a book by Ernest Hemingway and a few times just parked my truck at the corner of a playground and read until a few kids arrived. It turned out to be pretty exciting, about soldiers and war—in Spain instead of Vietnam, but I imagined Captain's son Thomas as a character.

I had it under my arm when I walked up to present Captain with lime sherbet.

"What you totin' there?" he asked.

I held it up. "It's for school."

"What's it say?"

"Captain, you must need glasses."

"I see plenty good," he said, turning away.

"I'm sorry," I said. "I didn't realize you couldn't . . ."

"Just tell me, what's it say!"

I read aloud the title: *For Whom the Bell Tolls.*

"School be startin' soon," Captain said. "You go and keep goin' long as you can."

"But I want to work too. There's a burger place, and after school I can make some extra money."

"Your Mama and Daddy sick?"

"No sir."

"You got a wife? Children? House?"

"I'm only sixteen!"

"Before you know it, son, you gonna have all those things, good and bad and won't be able to do nothin' but work. Right now, just like I used to tell my Thomas"—he reached out and thumped the book—"this the work you do."

I put the book back under my arm and returned to the truck. He waved me goodbye from the porch swing, rocking back and forth, dangling his legs like a little boy, spooning up his sherbet.

•

The next Monday Mr. Lewis stopped me while I was handing Reggie Douglas my orders and asked me to come to his office. On the way there we walked by the student from Forest Prep who looked the other way just like when he was in the truck, but somehow different now. I swallowed hard and wiped sweat from around my eyes with the sleeve of my T-shirt.

Mr. Lewis wasn't mean when he spoke. He didn't even raise his voice. He told me I was about to learn a hard lesson, and that getting fired when we were young sometimes saved us from making bigger mistakes when we were older, when losing a job could make a grown man with a family around his neck crumple up and weep. He shook my hand and told me good luck and showed me the door. I walked out of it and kept walking all the way to where the river began. I sat there all day watching the barges go by, and even a couple of skiffs that looked like Bobby Smit's.

If I went home too early, Daddy would be suspicious. It'd be better to tell him the next morning.

Twice I heard the pinging of ice cream truck bells. I clapped my hands over my ears. They kept on ringing inside my head.

Next thing I know I looked out over the water and storm clouds were building.

Far out in the Gulf of Mexico a tropical depression had begun, kicking up winds and rain. By that night, when I was home, it was called Tropical Storm Greta, and the TV weathermen, bored with endless summer, waved their hands excitedly at tracking charts and told us not to panic.

But no one could have been as excited as me.

As I tossed in bed I heard the storm churning right over us. By daybreak we had a foot of water in low-lying streets. Power lines were knocked out by fallen branches. The mayor asked residents, except in emergencies, not to drive.

Ice cream truck summer had come to an end.

"Sorry, son," Daddy consoled me.

"These things happen, Dad."

It got better. I started school, met a new girl, Sally, whose parents had moved from Pensacola, and took Cap's advice about not having an after-school job unless I really needed it. I thought of him, easy on his porch, licking his chops for ice cream. There was nothing to keep me from going to the convenience store and buying him a box myself, but there was plenty else to keep me busy.

The end of September turned dog-days hot and, miraculously, Mr. Lewis called saying he wanted to send the trucks out one last weekend.

"Did you know I used to be a high school football coach?" he said.

I told him I didn't.

"What happens when you fumble the ball?'

"You lose it."

"Who do you really let down?"

"The whole team."

"And next time out?"

I thought a moment. "Hang on to the ball? Yeah, next time out you hang on tight."

"One more chance, Rick."

I'd have jumped through the phone to thank him if I could.

My truck seemed to know the route without me the next day, rattling and clanging its way to Riverbend. I'd be stopping at Captain's just long enough to say hello and load him up with ice cream until the cold weather came.

Where was he, though?

Although it was ninety degrees again, there was no sign

of him outside the house, and a Thunderbird sat hulking in the driveway. I parked in front and sounded the bell. I saw the curtain draw back, then close. I beat the bell. The curtain opened again and the face at the window was a fair-complexioned, blonde woman.

"That must be Thomas's wife," I said to myself. "They're visiting from Germany!"

I took a full box of vanilla cups and made my way to the door. If this was Captain's family reunion, why not help with the party? When I knocked I was met by Thomas himself on the other side of the screen: a tall, broad-shouldered man dressed not in a uniform but a blue jean shirt.

"We don't care to buy anything," he said.

"But I stop here regularly."

"Thank you, but not today." He pushed the door shut.

"But I always bring Captain ice cream," I called out.

The door creaked back open and Thomas stood facing me again through the screen.

"I've heard all his great stories about ice cream. About Mr. A. O.'s creamery, about the time you had that high fever, about your mother eating that dish of strawberry."

Thomas turned and spoke over his shoulder in German. I heard his wife sigh and answer him.

"Daddy'd do anything for a little company," he said, "and there I was living two thousand miles away." He opened the screen some and shook his head slowly. "Daddy passed last week."

"Oh." I looked down not knowing what else to say and shifted the frigid box between my hands. I had never known anybody, while I was grown, who'd passed away. I was little when I lost my grandparents, but I never had the chance to hear their stories up close, spooning cold dessert, like I had Captain's. Their faces flashed in front of me, too.

"What you got there?" Thomas asked.

"Vanilla cups," I said, expecting to find Captain peering over his shoulder.

"Daddy liked those?"

"Sure he did."

He reached into his pocket. "Let me buy a few."

"But I always gave them to Captain. I mean, he'd tell me a story about ice cream, and then we'd talk."

"For real?"

"Every time."

Thomas chuckled. "What kind of stories?"

"You know, his ice cream ones."

"Oh, yeah, well"—he glanced again over his shoulder—"if you got a moment, I guess it'd be okay." He opened the screen wide. "You want to come on in? Greta's my wife, and she doesn't speak much English, but she likes ice cream and what else we got to do? Our flight's not until tomorrow."

They showed me to the kitchen table—I didn't let on I'd sat there before—and they pulled up their chairs and dug into their cups. As I began to tell them the stories about ice cream Captain had told me, Thomas moaned, laughed, shook his head.

"You must know all these by heart," I said.

He did not answer. I guess I never paid much attention to my Daddy's stories, either.

By the time I'd finished Thomas pressed twenty-five dollars into my palm, more than twice the value of the box of vanilla cups, which Greta went and stored in the freezer. When I tried to hand the money back, Thomas insisted I keep it.

"Just tell that one again about Daddy on Saturday nights. Tell it"—Thomas said—"for Greta."

I looked at the young woman with pale green eyes who understood not a word.

"Tell it," Thomas urged.

I recounted it one more time, watching Captain's son lean forward, hanging on every syllable. When it was over he shook my hand vigorously, and Greta even gave me a hug.

As I cranked up the truck, I figured that I'd started my job trying to make money selling chocolate-covereds and Nutty Buddies and Dreamsicles, but now I was being paid to spin tales. Down the steamy Alabama streets I drove, ringing the bell for Captain, who'd taught me how.

SEASHELL MOTEL

Lois Metzger

Cindy Fisher, whose motto at age sixteen was "To thine own self be true," lied to get her summer job.

Just before that summer, Mrs. Karpinsky, the guidance counselor at Cindy's high school in Queens, in New York City, gathered all the tenth graders in the school's big auditorium to tell them that a summer job would "broaden their horizons." Working her way through a tall pile of applications, Mrs. Karpinsky talked glowingly and unconvincingly about neighborhood restaurants, bakeries, small offices (Cindy'd been a file clerk two summers before—deadly experience), and city parks (Cindy had speared litter the previous summer; well, at least she'd been outdoors). As this year's pile of applications got smaller and smaller, Mrs. Karpinsky at some point mentioned that the Seashell Motel, down in Atlantic City, in New Jersey, was looking for a front desk clerk.

Cindy, sitting in the front row but way over to the left, where she was almost invisible, immediately raised her hand and called out, "I'll take that one!"

Mrs. Karpinsky squinted, located Cindy, walked over, and handed her the Seashell Motel form. And right away tried to take it back. "Oops," she said briskly, "So sorry. That's for my Queens College kids. You must be nineteen."

"I can do it," Cindy said.

"I'm sure you could, dear," said the suddenly soothing voice of Mrs. Karpinsky, who was not about to be thrown off course by this minor slip-up. "Don't you see, this job would entail living on your own, in a strange city . . ."

But Atlantic City's not strange! Cindy thought. Long before summer jobs, Cindy had been taken to Atlantic City every summer for two weeks, staying at the bustling, elegant, sun-drenched Traymore Hotel. The casinos weren't there then, she remembered. It always made Cindy smile, to think that the game Monopoly was based on Atlantic City— and that she got to stay at a real hotel on the real Boardwalk. Of course, the real city was a complicated grid of streets, not a simple square like the game. The streets runing parallel to the ocean all magically had the names of oceans and seas, while all the cross streets were named, far less spectacularly, after different states. In the game and in life, the closer to the ocean, the better the property. Pacific and Atlantic Avenues (green and yellow squares, and expensive, in Monopoly) were cheerful, festive streets with hotels and shops near the beach. Baltic and Mediterranean Avenues, twice as far from the ocean, were—well, not purple and cheap, as in the game, but very definitely seedy and cheap-looking. The Boardwalk itself, right along the ocean, was beautiful; Cindy loved taking motorized buggy rides on this wide wooden path that seemed to extend endlessly in both directions; and chewing tough, stretchy salt water taffy; and hearing the ocean roar all the time—the ocean, in Atlantic City, she had thought, seemed to be everywhere.

Cindy couldn't let the application out of her hands. "I'll

give it to my older sister," she told Mrs. Karpinsky. "She's nineteen."

"That's a fine idea," Mrs. Karpinsky said, brightening again. "I've had trouble filling that one."

Good, no competition, Cindy thought.

"And since when," said Charlotte, a friend of Cindy's, who was sitting behind her diagonally, "did your baby sister turn nineteen?"

"Since never mind," Cindy said with a grin.

When Cindy got home, she told her parents that this summer a new program would be sending lots of sixteen-year-old girls to hotels all up and down the east coast, where they would be well looked after by kindly hotel managers. "The school guidance counselor told me she was sure I was right for this job," Cindy explained. "She said it will broaden my horizons." Her parents looked impressed. So Cindy filled out the application form, writing down her age as "19" instead of "16." How easy! Just flip a single digit upside down!

Ocean view, right on Indiana Avenue, said the brochure for the Seashell Motel, which Cindy read on the bus to Atlantic City, that first weekend after the Fourth of July. *Experienced, conscientious staff.* It hadn't fazed Cindy to add a second fib to her application, inventing a summer at the Belle Heights Hotel, "unfortunately now no longer in business." Cindy scrutinized the photo of the front desk, of the smiling, well-groomed young man in a blazer and tie. Hmm, Cindy hadn't noticed that detail before. All she owned were gauzy skirts and flowing tops. She kept her frizzy, dark blond hair at waist length, and she didn't touch makeup.

Cindy got off the bus and into a taxi, proud that she'd packed light—only one large duffel bag. When she got off at Indiana Avenue and the Boardwalk, there was no Seashell Motel on the corner or even near it. Then, squinting, she spotted curvy letters on a rooftop several blocks inland: SEASHELL MOTEL.

The air smelled beach-y as Cindy walked; the sky felt low, right on her head; and the city, at least on Indiana Avenue, seemed sadder than she remembered, with many stores out of business or about to be. There was talk of building casinos someday—would that liven things up? If this was a real Monopoly game, Cindy decided, whoever held Indiana Avenue would lose.

Finally, on Arctic Avenue—omitted from the game, and halfway between the good oceans and the bedraggled ones— there it was, the Seashell Motel. Only three stories high (the Traymore had practically been a skyscraper), and modern, plain, square, beige. Ocean view? Maybe if you stood on the roof with a stepladder. Cindy couldn't even hear the waves— so the ocean wasn't everywhere in Atlantic City, after all.

The lobby was all windows; Cindy felt as if she'd stepped inside an ice cube with couches and carpeting. To her left was an unimpeded view of a parking lot; to her right was the front desk (*her* front desk!) with a clean-cut young man behind it. Well, the brochure was accurate about something, because he looked almost exactly like the picture—handsome, short brown hair slicked back, blue blazer, tie. About twenty-two years old—three years older than the age Cindy was supposed to be. All the boys Cindy liked in Queens had long shaggy hair and wore tie-dyed T-shirts. But would Cindy be attracted to this guy if she were nineteen? Should she flash him a big smile?

"Welcome," the young man said, and flashed her a big smile. A professional one. "Room for the weekend?"

"My name is—Cynthia Fisher," Cindy said, a bit hesitantly. Cynthia sounded so much more mature. I'm Cynthia now, Cindy told herself firmly. "I'll be working here—with you, I guess."

The young man raised an eyebrow at her. "Not really," he said.

"Why?" she stammered. "Why not really?"

"You look a little young, that's all," he tossed off.

Cindy heard a kind of alarm in her head, almost like a fire drill at school. *You're fired!* said a voice inside her, a voice she'd never heard before. *Even before your first day on the job.* It's the clothes, Cindy told herself. The hair. I'll have to dress old, wear my hair old—in short, *be* old.

But first things first. What was it about a fire drill, the most important thing? Stay calm. "So you think I look young," Cindy said. "Why, thank you." That was what Cindy's mother always said when people told her she looked young. Maybe she sounded too old? "I'm nineteen," she added. "Honestly. This is actually my third job." But she didn't say anything about how expert she was at putting papers in alphabetical order, or at spearing litter with a tall, sharply pointed pole.

"Fine," he said. "Believe me, I don't care if you're nineteen or ninety." And he added something about "money wouldn't care, either way."

"Money?" Cindy asked, wondering what this had to do with her forty-dollar-a-week salary, plus a free room and meals in the kitchen.

"Michael Munn—our manager. Munny, get it?"

"Oh," Cindy said.

"You won't see Munny much. Mostly he works the desk at night. His girlfriend manages the singer Jack Jones—you heard of him?" Cindy hadn't. But she nodded. Cynthia, of course, would have heard of Jack Jones. "He sings at the Steel Pier, the one with the diving horse. Actually, the horse isn't too willing. Some guy has to push it. It's more of a sliding horse."

That sounded just awful, but Cindy didn't say anything.

What if this guy thought the diving horse was cool? What if, at nineteen, she might think so, too?

"I'm Tim Chamberlain—studying hotel management at LSU, Louisiana State University to you folks up north." That was when Cindy heard the accent—distinctly southern. She'd never met a boy from the South before. See what a good idea this summer was! Broadening her horizons! "That's why I'm here; LSU places us at the best resorts." He sounded pleased. Cindy noticed fifty slots for keys; about half were empty. Behind Tim was a switchboard. In all this time, no guests had entered or left the lobby or even called. "Are you in college?" Tim asked her.

"High school." Cindy cleared her throat, stalling for time. Why hadn't she come up with a good cover story before now? Why had she assumed no one would ask her anything? "I mean, I finished high school last year. This year in college—Queens College—I'm studying parks, city parks. Park management."

"You like it?"

"Oh, tremendously." The fire drill alarm in Cindy's head wouldn't turn off. She might have to go on lying all afternoon, like a stereo needle stuck in a record groove—nineteen years old, knew all about Jack Jones, acing park management at Queens College, and what else? But suddenly it was over:

"Munny told me to put you in Room Two-twelve," Tim said. "Don't blame me if I got here last week and snared Two-sixteen. It's twice the size."

"That's okay. I don't need a lot of room."

"Don't you ever smile?" he asked her.

Cindy just blinked at him. Back home, she and Charlotte laughed all the time. But she wasn't about to start laughing here. Too risky.

Tim sighed. "If it's the last thing I do," he said, "I'll make you laugh." Cindy wasn't sure whether or not this was a good goal. "My girlfriend says I can make anyone laugh."

"You have a girlfriend?"

"Going steady three years."

Cindy let out a big sigh. She didn't have to worry about flirting, and flirting back, and who-knew-what-else with twenty-two-year-old Tim Chamberlain.

Tim misinterpreted the sigh and smiled a sorry-to-disappoint-you smile. "After you get settled in," he said, "Munny will show you the ropes."

So I can hang myself? Cindy wondered. "I need to pick up a few things first," she said. A few things? New clothes, makeup, sensible shoes—a whole new self.

Small as it was, Room 212 was bigger than the tiny room Cindy shared back home with her baby sister—and now this queen-sized bed, nightstand, tiny refrigerator, wooden bureau, small color television, and striped wallpaper that was sort of beige and yellow were all hers. This is where Cindy can be Cindy, she thought, placing her three favorite books on the nightstand (*Catcher in the Rye, To Kill a Mockingbird,* and *A Separate Peace*). It was Cindy's first summer away from home, except for sleep-away camp, where she was never alone. She unpacked all her inappropriate clothing, looked at it, and then stuffed it all right back into her duffel bag.

Cindy stood behind the front desk with Munny, her hair pulled back, wearing a sleeveless white linen blouse, navy skirt, and mid-heeled navy pumps (bringing her height up to five feet ten inches). She could actually feel the makeup on her skin, lipstick on her lips. Get used to it, she told herself.

Munny, a tall, cheerful guy with curly brown hair and circles under his eyes, told her, "Besides Tim, the rest of the staff is a few guys in the kitchen, a couple of bellhops, and a couple ladies in Housekeeping—awful sweet, but no *habla* much *Ingles.*"

Cindy looked out at the lobby from the front desk. She felt like a new teacher surveying a still-empty classroom, except that instead of orderly desks and chairs there were only some awkwardly arranged and shapeless pale blue upholstered couches. What could I possibly tell anybody? Cindy asked herself. What are these couches supposed to be learning?

"You either work the day shift, from eight in the morning to four in the afternoon," Munny told her, "or the swing shift, from four in the afternoon until midnight. Or the graveyard shift, from midnight to eight; I work that shift myself a lot. Sometimes you have to work two shifts in a row." The switchboard buzzed—Room 207 lit up. "You know the switchboard, right?" he asked her.

"It's a little different from the one at the Belle Heights Hotel," she told him. "Could you show me?"

Munny put on a phone headset and picked up a black wire with a metal tip and clicked it into Room 207. "Good afternoon, Seashell Motel," he said, "How may I help you? Yes, of course. I'll send it up right away." Munny yanked out the black wire. "Now I'll call Housekeeping and ask them to deliver towels and toilet paper to the gentleman in Room Two-oh-seven. The usual, right?"

"Right," Cindy said,

"In the morning, when you do your wake-up calls, don't get upset if people get mad at you, just remind them they asked for the call. When people check out, get payment right away, cash or credit card. When people check in, make sure you don't rent the same room twice."

"Oh, I'd never do that."

Munny didn't seem to have heard. "And keep an eye out for skippers."

Cindy's alarm went off again. Should she know this? "Skippers?" she asked, as if it were a word on the tip of her tongue.

"People who try to sneak out without paying. Let me know if you have any other questions, or talk to Tim if I'm not around. You heard of Jack Jones?"

"Yes," Cindy said with confidence.

"His career is really taking off—my girlfriend is his manager. I may co-manage him someday." *You won't see Munny much,* Tim had told Cindy. She began constructing in her head the Munny she would describe when her parents called—a Munny as attentive as a chaperon, who sat down with her every afternoon to find out how things were going. The switchboard buzzed again and the real-life Munny plugged in a wire. "Good afternoo—oh, no, sir, I haven't forgotten about you. Towels and toilet paper right away!"

There was one worker Munny had neglected to mention. The guy who came in every Thursday to fill up the Pepsi machine in the lobby. Long dark hair, sea-green eyes, and neon T-shirts. Sometimes he sneaked Cindy a couple cans of Orange Slice before loading up the machine. Cal, he said his name was, age sixteen and a half, and he lived just off Tennessee Avenue (an orange square in the game and a pretty decent block in the real city). Not Cynthia's type, but sometimes, during one of Cindy's many solitary, off-duty hours out on the pale peach-colored sand, she imagined sweet, romantic walks on the beach with Cal, watching the waves curl over themselves and slide up onto the sand.

And there were guests, after all, real live guests who marched up to Cindy and never guessed that she wasn't exactly what she appeared to be—a well-groomed nineteen-year-old front-desk clerk. She assigned them rooms, processed their credit cards, handled their calls. Only two of them stayed in Cindy's mind—the cute four-year-old girl who gathered a whole pillowcaseful of seashells on the beach and then dumped them on the lobby carpet—the only time the place truly became the Seashell Motel. And a mostly unseen man in Room 333 who asked for a wake-up call at eight but at eight asked her to call back in twenty minutes, and at eight-twenty said the same thing, and kept it up for two hours. The last time he didn't even answer his phone, and Cindy was suddenly sure he was a skipper. But he was just on his way downstairs to check out. He looked exhausted.

During Cindy's second week, working a graveyard shift, Tim told her that the gentleman in Room 111 requested a five a.m. wake-up call.

"Good morning, Seashell Motel!" Cindy said cheerfully, as the sky outside the lobby turned orangy red. "This is your five o'clock wake-up call!"

"Are you out of your mind?" the man said, and slammed down the phone.

Tim—trying to make Cindy laugh.

"You'll get me fired!" Cindy complained to Tim at the end of her shift.

"Munny won't care. He appreciates a good joke."

Cindy must still be on the far side of a sense of humor that embraced nineteen-year-olds and all adults.

When work got slow, Cindy flipped through magazines, sitting on a high stool behind the desk. If she ever caught herself wondering whether she'd be better off back home stabbing litter, she straightened her shoulders and touched up her makeup. The ladies in Housekeeping grinned at her, and she smiled back politely; the guys in the kitchen joked with her; she also smiled back politely. One of the bellhops, Victor, showed Cindy pictures of his eight kids, spilling all over each other in their backyard, but when he asked her about herself, she clammed up. Cindy's new theory was that she could hold only so many lies in her head; she was afraid she'd start forgetting some of the important ones if she tried to pile in more.

One particularly slow afternoon, about a month after Cindy had started working at the Seashell Motel, Cal slipped her three cans of Slice and said, "Want to go to the Steel Pier tonight? I can't afford Jack Jones, but we can just walk around."

Cindy straightened her shoulders and tried to sound like an older sister. "Yes, sure, that sounds like fun," she said. "But no diving horse."

"No diving horse!" Cal promised. "I'll pick you up later."

The night was humid; if Cindy hadn't tied back her hair, it would have spread out like a fan. Cindy wished Atlantic City were the way she remembered, bright and magical and fun, but it had gotten so run down, even on the blue-square, top-of-the-line Boardwalk. The solitary types hanging out at the pier at night looked far worse than anybody she'd ever seen in Queens. And how could so few people generate so much litter? Loud music blared noisily and scratchily from several different places. The ocean was still beautiful, but the frame around the picture was falling to pieces.

Cal walked alongside her in faded jeans and a white T-shirt and said, "Is college very different from high school?"

Out of nowhere, Cindy remembered something she'd heard somewhere. "College is high school with ashtrays."

Cal laughed loudly. He was dazzled by her, an older woman. Would he have liked Cindy? "I can't wait to get out of high school," he said.

Cindy knew the feeling. "I remember," she said. "But looking back on it, high school wasn't so bad."

They came to a fun house, and Cal said, "Want to go in the Hall of Mirrors?"

"Sounds ... delightful," she said, something Cindy would never say. Cindy herself hadn't been inside a place like that in ten years. It was dark and sparkly, and she saw Cal and herself, thousands of them, reflected in mirror after mirror.

Cal, exactly Cindy's height when she wore her sandals but a little shorter now that she was in heels, took hold of Cindy's shoulders and leaned up to kiss her. Cindy saw it thousands of times.

Cindy wanted so badly to kiss him. What a sweet, romantic moment in the city she'd loved so much as a kid! But she was Cynthia now, a girl with a fire drill in her head. And Cynthia pulled back.

Cal let go right away. "I get it," he said, smiling gently. "Too young. Hey, it's okay."

Cindy felt sick to her stomach, seasick on dry land. This whole Atlantic City summer had been such a bad idea! She hadn't simply turned a digit upside down—she'd turned her whole self upside down!

"Don't look so sad," Cal told her. "We can still take a walk together sometime, okay?"

"Let's just go," Cindy said, turning to leave; for a moment she couldn't see where the exit was. She felt trapped, locked in with thousands of versions of herself, not one of them real. Then she and Cal together walked very slowly forward, bumping into mirrors a couple of times but finally finding the real, the true way out.

"Have fun robbing the cradle?" Tim asked Cindy, as she entered the lobby. When he saw Cindy's face, he said, "I'm sorry—Cal's a nice guy. What's a few years, anyway?"

Plenty, Cindy thought. If you haven't lived them yet.

Cindy had to work a double shift the next week. She watched

the sky go from the deep gray to purply black. At midnight, she headed upstairs to bed—and slept until three o'clock the next day, Thursday. She headed out to the beach, avoiding Cal and Tim both, staying out all afternoon and quite late into the evening. She was practically the only person there. The waves were enormous, the sky too gray and dark. A hot dog vendor told her that a hurricane was coming.

Back in the Seashell Motel, Cindy opened the door to her room and thought she heard the sound of a television. Must be somebody in the next room, she figured. Then she looked inside. At the man in her bed.

Thunderous fire alarms! Maybe, at nineteen, she'd know how to handle this. . . .

"What do you want?" the man said, as Cindy just stood there, staring. He was skinny and had a stubbly beard and was wearing striped boxer shorts, nothing more, and watching a Western.

"This is my room!" Cindy said, sounding like a little girl. *The place where I'm Cindy, the only place.*

"The guy at the desk gave me this room," he said, not bothering to pull a sheet over himself or anything. "I paid cash." But Cindy felt a little calmer. She could see he wasn't a mass murderer or anything. Just a guy in the wrong room, like a misfiled piece of paper.

"You see, I work here," Cindy said. "I live here. Those are my clothes in the drawers." Or, rather, Cynthia's clothes, she thought distractedly.

"I wondered about that. I thought the last person left a lot of stuff and the cleaning lady didn't get around to it."

Cindy picked up the phone.

"Good evening," came Tim's cheerful voice. "Is everything satisfactory in Room Two-twelve?"

"I can't believe you did this," Cindy said.

She could feel Tim smile. "He's a harmless old duffer. He stayed here the week before you came. Don't you think it's kind of funny?"

Was it kind of funny? Or kind of horrible? Was Tim an irritating practical joker or a friend trying to make her laugh? Cindy absolutely didn't know what to think or how to feel, where nobody could even see.

Into her silence, Tim said, "I'll be right up."

Cindy waited for Tim out in the hall. As he got off the elevator, he told her, "I'll help move the guy to a room on the third floor." Tim entered Cindy's room. The man had put on pants and a shirt. "Your books?" Tim asked Cindy.

"No," Cindy said. Those books, her favorite books, were kid books. "I found them in this room my first day here—we can get rid of them." Even Cindy's room had become Cynthia's.

The following night, the hurricane hit. Cindy had never heard anything like it. The wind moaned—literally moaned, a long, low groan, like somebody dreading a trip to the dentist. Rain hit the window hard, sideways. From her bed, in her flannel nightgown, Cindy lay awake, listening.

Her phone rang.

Cindy figured it was her parents, seeing if she was all right in the hurricane. But it was Cal. "I'm downstairs," he said. "I thought you might like to go for a walk."

"You mean, now?" Cindy said, shocked. "Take a walk in the hurricane?"

She could feel him smiling. "You'll see, it's so beautiful."

"It's so crazy!"

"Not when you know what you're doing. I've lived here my whole life. I know what I'm doing."

Cindy didn't say anything. She definitely wanted to go. Did Cynthia?

"Put on a bathing suit and sandals," Cal said. "I'll wait for you in the lobby."

Cindy hung up, and put on a black one-piece bathing suit. She'd worn it earlier, so it was still a little damp.

Cal had a towel around his shoulders and he wore dark blue trunks and sandals. He took hold of her hand, and his hand told her, *You'll see, I know what I'm doing.* Tim was too busy taping up the lobby windows even to notice them leave.

Outside, the moan of the wind was much louder, almost deafening. They headed towards the Boardwalk, getting soaked within moments. Soon the water, though warm, was waist-high on the flooded streets. Telephone poles drifted by; Cal carefully, expertly steered Cindy out of the way.

No alarms went off in Cindy's head, despite the fact that at any moment she might be hit by a falling telephone pole, or get electrocuted, or drown, or find herself swept away, never to be seen again. For the first time all summer, in the middle of all this real danger, Cindy, here with Cal, felt truly calm and safe.

When they reached the Boardwalk—looking more like a Sidewalk now, because it was right at the level of the still-rising water—they stopped. The sky and the sea were the same dark gray; you couldn't tell where one began and the other left off. Mrs. Karpinsky had never said that broadening your horizons would mean not even seeing the horizon. And Cindy, looking out at the ocean—the ocean that was everywhere—saw something she'd never seen before. The waves didn't act like waves. They didn't curl over and come to the shore; instead they coupled off and slapped together sideways, like hands clapping.

"What do you think?" Cal said. "I told the truth, didn't I?"

"Cal," Cindy suddenly had to say, practically shouting to be heard, "I'm not really who you think I am."

"You're not?" Cal said.

Cindy felt flooded—not by the water but by every lie she'd told that summer; there was a moan, not from the hurricane, but from deep inside her. "I'm only sixteen years old," she confessed, expecting the ocean to swallow her whole. "So you see, the way I dress, the way I act, even the way I feel . . . I'm just one big lie, inside and out!"

Cindy could see this information swirling around Cal's head for several long moments. Finally he smiled at her. "That's so brave of you!" he said, with more admiration than he'd shown Cynthia. "I'm sixteen—I've never done anything like that, not even left home for a night."

"I don't feel brave," Cindy said, frowning. "I just feel stuck. I told the hotel I was nineteen so they'd hire me. And I told my parents I was in a chaperoned program for sixteen-year-olds so they'd let me go. I got in way over my head." Almost literally, she thought, with water up to her middle.

Cal held her hand tighter. "So you're brave, and also a little foolish, too," he said. "When will you tell your parents?"

Cindy frowned some more. "I didn't—I mean, I wasn't planning to—" But Cindy knew she had to tell them. It was like packing and unpacking—part of going home. Will my parents lock me in my room for the rest of my life? she wondered. Maybe she deserved it. Or maybe, long after their initial shock, anger, and dismay, they might actually admire her a little—for pulling it off, for trying on a whole new self for size. Or at least they'd want to help her get good at getting from sixteen to nineteen. Finding out what they really felt would be part of that, too, wouldn't it? "I'll tell them everything," Cindy said, "but not just yet." In a month, she thought, after hurricane season, when the leaves turn burnt colors and I've had several long moments to think about it, too.

Meanwhile, there was the rest of the summer to get through. The moan of the hurricane was getting louder.

"We'd better head back," Cal said. "It's rougher now—window-popping time."

Sure enough, back at the Seashell Motel, a window in the lobby, despite the tape, had shattered; seawater poured in. Tim, at the switchboard, was calling Munny. Cal and Cindy grabbed mops. Look, Cindy thought, the brochure wasn't a complete lie: *Ocean view, right on Indiana Avenue. Experienced, conscientious staff.*

THE BASEBALL GLOVE

Víctor Martínez

One summer my brother Bernardo, or Nardo, as we used to call him, flipped through more jobs than a thumb through a deck of cards. He was a busboy, a dishwasher, then a parking attendant, and, finally, a patty-turner for some guy who never seemed to be in his hamburger stand more than ten minutes at a time (my mom believed he sold marijuana, or did some other illegal shamelessness). Nardo lost the first job for not showing up regular enough, the next for showing up too regular (the boss hated his guts). The last job lost him when the owner of the stand packed up unexpectedly and left for Canada with a whole month of his wages.

The job he misses most, though, was when he worked as a busboy for the Bonneville Lakes Golf and Catering Service. He says it was the only time he ever got to touch elbows with the rich people. The parties they catered served free daiquiris, hard drinks, and iced beer (really iced, in big barrels choking with ice). In some, like the one he got fired from, they passed out tickets for juicy prizes like motorcycles, TV sets, stereos, and snow skis. This particular party featured a six-piece band that once opened for Jimmy Durante and a great, huge dance floor so the "old fogies" (as my brother called them) could get drunk and make fools out of themselves. The way he tells it, you would think he did that man a favor working for him.

It turns out he and a guy named Randy took off their busboy jackets and began daring each other to get a ticket and ask a girl to dance. Hell, Nardo said, the guy bet he wouldn't, and he bet he would, and after a two-dollar pledge Nardo steered for the ticket lady.

"I could've hashed it around a bit, you know, Manny," he told me. "I could've double- and triple-dared the guy a couple of times over, then come up with a good excuse. But that ain't my style." Instead he tapped the guy's fingers real smooth and walked up to the ticket lady. She looked out from behind the large butcher-paper-covered table at the blotches of pasta sauce on his black uniform pants and white shirt—which were supposed to look clean along with the catering service's light orange busboy jacket, but didn't—and said, "Ah, what the hell," and tore him a tag.

Then, before the little voice nagging inside him could talk some sense, he asked the nearest girl for a dance. She was close to his age and had about a million freckles and enough wire in her mouth to run a toy train over. They stumbled around the dance floor until the band mercifully grinded to a stop. She looked down at his arm kind of shy-like, and said, "You dance real nice."

Now my brother had what you'd call a sixth sense. *Es muy vivo,* as my grandmother used to say about kids born that way, and with Nardo it was pretty much a scary truth, because he could duck trouble better than a boxer could duck a right cross. He made hairline escapes from belt-whippings and scoldings, just by not being around when punishment came through the door. So I believed him when he said something ticklish crawled over his shoulder when he looked across the dance floor, and in front of the bandleader who was about to read an announcement over the mike, he saw his boss, Mr. Baxter—and boy, was he steamed!

Mr. Baxter owned the catering service, and sometimes, my brother said, the way he'd yell at the busboys, it was like he owned them too. Mr. Baxter didn't say anything, just pointed to the door, then at Nardo, and wrote a big, imaginary X across Nardo's chest. Just like that, he was fired.

"Don't you ever get braces, Manny," my brother said, as if that were the lesson he learned.

At first he refused to go to the fields (although my mother insisted that my father was insisting), not because of pride, although he would have used that excuse at the beginning if he could have gotten away with it, but because like anyone else, he didn't like sweating over clods of dirt under a 105–degree sun.

That summer was a scorcher, maybe the worst in all the years our family lived in that desert, which our town would've been if the irrigation water pumped in from the Sierras was turned off. I could tell how searing it was by the dragged-out way my mom's roses looked every morning after I watered them. The water didn't seem to catch hold, and the roses only sighed a moment before the sun sucked up even that little breather, leaving the stems to sliver, curl up, and turn ashen.

Everyone else in my family worked, and it was hard to remain inconspicuous when my sister Magda always returned home from the laundry slumped over from feeding bedsheets all day into a monster steam press. I hustled fruit with my Uncle Louie, who owned a '58 Ford pickup. Together we sold melons, apples, peaches, oranges, whatever was in season, from door to door. But Uncle Louie hurt his leg tripping over some tree roots in our front yard, and it was all swollen blue and tender at the ankle. For a while, he couldn't walk at all except to hobble on one leg to the fridge or lean over to change channels on our black-and-white. He didn't go to the doctor because he figured nothing was broke, so why pay good money to some old fart just to write something on a piece of paper.

Anyway, the only one not working was my brother Nardo. But after a while, no one really expected anything from him. The truth of the matter was that he was just plain lazy. Whether one tried threats, scoldings, or even shaming (which my mom tried almost every other day), nothing worked. We all gave it a shot, but none more than my dad. He'd yell and stomp around a little space of anger that he'd cut out in our living room, declaring to the walls what a good-for-nothing son he had. He'd even dare Nardo, sometimes, to at least be a man and get up off his ass and go join the Army.

My dad's English wasn't so good. Some words he just couldn't say right. Instead of saying "watch," he would say "wash," and for "stupid," he would slip in a bit of Spanish, "estupid." But when he said "ass," or "ounce," stretching the S with a long, lingering slowness, there was pure acid in his teeth.

"If only Bernardo had jus' whuan ounss, whuan ounss . . ." my dad would say, making the tiniest measure between his thumb and forefinger, but using a voice the size of our entire block.

After a while everybody gave up on poor Nardo. It was too bad, really, especially for my dad, who truly believed that with enough yelling and jumbling of the veins around his neck he could correct the error that was his son. When he finally woke up to the fact that it wasn't ever going to happen, his heart crumbled into bitter, disappointed pieces. From then on my dad acted like Nardo was just empty space.

Nardo, for his part, stayed home lifting weights, doing push-ups and sit-ups, and tenderly nursing any piddling little pimple worth a few hours of panic. He was a nut for health and fanatical about his handsome looks. He must've combed his hair at least a hundred times a day in the mirror.

I wasn't like Nardo at all, and my dad reminded me of it every time my brother's name boiled up from his lip. I suppose fourteen years of not knowing what, besides work, was expected from a Mexican was enough to convince me that I wouldn't pass from this earth without putting in a lot of days. I was of my Uncle Louie's line of useful blood. All his life, no matter what the job, my uncle worked like a man trying to fill all his tomorrows with a full day's work. He didn't like sitting on the couch, didn't like TV one bit, never laughed at Skelton or got sentimental over Andy of Mayberry—mostly because he didn't understand them very well. The first chance my uncle got, he started fumbling about the house fixing sockets and floor trim, painting lower shelves and screwing legs back onto tables and chairs. He was a genius with clay tiles, and during that time he and my dad laid down the kitchen floor, which is still there to this day.

But with my Uncle Louie crippled, I was empty as a Coke bottle. I needed money for school clothes and paper supplies. I also wanted a baseball glove so bad a sweet hurt bloomed inside a hollow place in my stomach every time I thought about it. Baseball had a grip on my fantasies and wouldn't let go. There was an outfielder's mitt in the window of Duran's Department Store that kept me dreaming downright dangerous, diving Willie Mays catches. I decided to stir up Nardo to see if we couldn't go pick some chili peppers.

"You can buy some weights," I said a bit too enthusiastically, making him suspicious right off the bat.

He looked up at me from the middle of a push-up.

"You think I'm lazy, huh?"

"No," I lied.

"Yeah, you do. You think I'm lazy," he said, breathing tight as he pushed.

"I said no!"

"Yeah, you do!" He forced air out of his lungs, then got up miserably and wiped his hands. "But that's awright, college boy, if you think I'm lazy. Everybody else does."

He started picking at a sliver in his palm.

"I'm not really lazy, you know. I've been working."

He began biting for the sliver now, moving his elbow up and down like a wing, trying to get a better tooth on it.

"If you want me to go with you, I'll go, if that's what you want. But I'm telling you right now, if it gets hot, I'm quitting."

With that miracle we woke up the next morning, borrowed my uncle's primered pickup (which Nardo knew how to drive despite the tricky gearshift), and got some cans from our dad, who was pretty cheery over me getting Nardo out of hibernation. He practically put a birthday ribbon on the large brimmed hats from Mexico he gave us to protect us from the sun.

When we arrived at the chili field, the wind through the window of the pickup was burning warm on our shirtsleeves. Already the sky was beginning to hollow out, the clouds rushing toward the rim of the horizon like even they knew the sun would soon be the center of a boiling pot.

The foreman, wearing a pale yellow shirt with a black leather vest and cowboy boots curling back almost to his ankles, refused at first to hire us, saying I was too young, that it was too late (most fieldworkers got up while it was still dark), and besides, all the rows had been taken hours ago. On top of that we looked too much like kids strolling out for a picnic. He laughed at the huge lunch bag bulging under Nardo's arm.

Although he could fake disappointment better than anybody I knew, deep down I figured Nardo wanted to give picking chilies a try. But a good excuse was a good excuse, and any excuse was better than quitting, so Nardo didn't hesitate and hurriedly threw his can in the back of the pickup. He made a flourish to open the door, and seeing him so spunky and bouncing, I couldn't help but think it nothing less than pure torture when the foreman said that fortunately for us, there was a scrawny row no one wanted next to the road.

The foreman must have thought it an enormous joke giving us that row because he chuckled and called us over with a sneaky offer of his arm, as if to share a secret.

"Vamos muchachos, aquí hay un surco muy bueno que pueden piscar," he said, gesturing down at some limp branches.

The row had a coat of white pesticide dust and exhaust fumes so thick I knew our hands would get stained right away. The leaves were sparse and shriveled, dying for oxygen. Even the plants slanted from the road as though trying to hustle away from the passing traffic of people and trucks.

My brother shrugged. His luck gone, there was not much else to do. The foreman hung around a while to make sure we knew which peppers to pick and which to leave, not that it mattered in that row.

We had been picking for about an hour when the sun began scalding the backs of our hands, leaving a pocket of heat like a small animal crawling around between our shirts and skin. My fingers began to stiffen; it seemed forever before I reached the center of my can. Nardo, on the other hand, topped his can before I did, patted the chilies down, and lifted it over his shoulder, setting his rock of an arm solid against his cheek.

"I'm gonna get my money and buy me a soda," he said, and strode off over the rows toward the weighing area, carefully swishing his legs through the plants. I limped behind him, straining with my half-filled can of lungless chili peppers.

The weighing area wasn't anything special, just a tripod with a scale hook hanging from the center. People brought their cans and sagging burlap sacks and formed a line. After the scale pointer flipped and settled, heaving with the sack's weight, the sacks were unsewn and the peppers were dumped onto a table bed where slits between the slat-boards let the mixed-in dirt and leaves sift through. There was a line of older women and young girls, some with handkerchiefs masking their faces, standing along the sides cleaning and kneading the chilies through the chute at the end. When a sack was stuffed, one of the foremen unhooked it from the nails and sewed up the opening. Then he stacked it on a pile near a waiting truck, whose driver lay asleep in the cab with his boots sticking out the window, blurring in the waves of heat.

Standing near the table bed was sheer hell. Dried leaves and the angry scent of freshly broken chili peppers made my eyes flare and my nose dribble a mustache across my lip. No matter how hard I tried to keep my breath calm, I kept coughing and choking as if someone had stuffed a crushed ball of sandpaper down my throat. I wondered how the women were able to stand it, even with the handkerchiefs.

The only good thing about the weighing area, really, was that they paid a minute after they announced your load. This lured families and workers from Mexico needing quick cash for rent payments or emergency food, and people like me who had baseball mitts to buy. It also brought business to a burrito truck behind the scales owned by the labor contractor. It sold everything from tacos, chili beans, and egg burritos to snow cones and ice cream bars. The prices, though, made my brother complain loud: "You know how much I paid for this!" he exclaimed, when out of earshot of the foreman. "Eighty-five cents! Eighty-five cents for a damn soda! And it's one of those cheap jobs to top it off, no fizzle or nothing."

We picked steadily on, but by noon both Nardo and I were burnt out and a good sprint away from the nearest picker. Farther up, under where the clouds were like water boiling on the horizon, there was a staggered string of men working two rows apiece.

"They're wetbacks," my brother said as explanation. "They pick like their goddamned lives depended on it."

I looked over at the Mexican working the four rows next to ours and nodded agreement. The man used two cans, trading handfuls from one to the other. He went up two rows, then down two others, greeting us occasionally on his return with a smile and a shy wave. To save time, he placed sacks every twenty feet or so, and every half hour he'd pour a loaded can into the closest one. Behind him, three sacks already lay fat and tightly sewn. We eyed him, fascinated by his quickness.

"Maybe that's what we should do," I suggested.

Nardo shook his head. "Are you crazy?" he asked with conviction. "It'll take us the whole damn day just to fill one lousy sack."

He was right. We weren't really a threat to pass anyone. We stopped too much, my brother to eye the girls heading for the weigher, and I to watch the man and compare hands. His were wings in a blur of wonder, mine were stirring a pot of warm honey. He kept me mesmerized the whole morning with the way the nerves around his arm twitched as he shifted from plant to plant, his knees out like a triangle, tilting first one way, then another. He was a whirlwind gathering up cans and empty burlap sacks. He could've been a terrific shortstop, I thought, as I marveled at him, almost forgetting my own tiredness, noticing that he never seemed to tire, never seemed to rise much above the plant but hid inside the quivering leaves until with one flickering toss, a rain of peppers would shower the air and drop into his can. I was eyeing him when my brother tapped me on the shoulder.

"Look what's coming," he said, pointing his chin at a van creeping up the road. Cars had been insulting us with dust and fumes all morning, so when I saw how carefully the van approached, like a dog sneaking up on a bush, I knew something was wrong.

The van was green, a dim, starved-for-light green, like the leaves on our row. It had no markings. Its windows were open, and the man behind the wheel had his head out searching for something in the rows.

Suddenly people began to stand up, licking the air and stretching like they were peering over a wall. There was fast talking in Spanish and frenzied commotion as fifty or so people all at once jumped up and started running. They didn't even bother going through the furrows in scissor steps like Nardo had done, but ran in waves, trampling over the plants and tipping over cans. Those who were the last to react brought up the rear. They steadied their hats with one hand while their quickly snapped-up coats thrashed in the other.

I still didn't know what was happening. My first impulse was to run, but then I saw three more vans and a large labor bus pop out of a narrow road in the cornfield bordering ours, and I knew that the Immigration had come for the people.

No one had seen the other vans position themselves at points along the cornfield. The people just ran wildly in panic toward them as if their first instinct was to hide inside the stalks. The quicker ones got caught almost at once, their paths cut off by officers holding out their arms. They surrendered without a word. The slower ones veered off into the open spaces of the cordon and dove into the corn. Most were caught in the first sweep, except for the ones who ducked under the arms of the officers and made it down the road. But they, too, were quickly run down by another van and escorted inside.

The few who managed to hide inside the cornfield seemed

to have gotten away, and we all cheered and waved our arms as if our side had won. Some of us jeered at the officers, my brother Nardo the loudest. Everyone quieted down, though, when some of the officers formed a line along the field and disappeared into the stalks. A while later, they came out yanking on the shirt collars of those we thought had gotten away. Everybody sighed and said nothing.

The foreman who had given us the scraggly row and who was also the contractor rushed over to see what was going on. He took off in a huff saying "son-ova-beeches" and worse. I thought he was going to cuss those immigration guys off, but instead he stood by, meekly watching the officers corral the people before loading them into the vans. I tried to find the Mexican on the row next to ours, but I couldn't see him. I hoped he had gotten away.

The officer who looked like he was in charge approached the foreman and said something we could not make out, but it sounded like a scolding. Then the foreman came back and knelt down by the water tank.

"Damn son-ova-beeches," he said again, taking off his hat and raising dust as he slapped it against his pants leg. He poured himself some water and glared over at the immigration officers as they packed the people in and roared off in a growing cloud of dust. A crowd of us stood around covering our eyes, but none of us bothered to go back to work.

When the air cleared, a man appeared at the spot where the vans had assembled. He was an older man with a white stubble beard and a long, slightly darker mustache. He tottered back, nursing his right knee. At first I thought maybe he had gotten away, but then someone recognized him and laughed derisively.

"Hey, Joe, you're not a wetback. You're a *bracero*."

Joe came slowly over and took off his hat and covered his stomach as if he'd been caught naked. He shrugged an apology and said he couldn't help it, when everyone else began to run he got so scared and excited that he ran too. He looked down at his legs as if they had betrayed him. He said the Immigration let him go as soon as they saw he had too much meat on his bones to be a wetback. Everyone laughed. Then a family, whose befuddled uncle he was, came over and led him away. My brother and I laughed too, but for some reason I thought he was the best man in the whole field.

Of the twenty or so people left, everyone claimed they encouraged the Mexicans not to run. They said Immigration usually doesn't go inside the fields to check for green cards unless they have a good reason. If you acted like a citizen, sometimes you could fool them. None of those ungratefuls took them at their word, though, and for that they had only themselves to blame.

One of the listeners, a tall pimple-faced guy with blotched cheeks and the skin of a fig, only paler, shouted out, "*Pinches gavachos* don't give a damn about harassing us. *Gavachos* do what they want."

He walked away, not even waiting for a response or picking up any cans or equipment. Everybody watched as he slammed the door of his rusty Buick and drove away.

"I guess he came alone," Bernardo said musingly, then more alert, "We can pick any row we want, now." With the back of his wrist, he rubbed his eyes, even though the dust had died down.

"That guy's crazy. Those people don't live here, anyway," said a fat, moist-face guy with tight, bunched-in cheeks and pants that settled unevenly around his waist. When he walked, one of his legs looked shorter than the other. He went over to one of the rows a Mexican had been picking and lifted up a pair of old shoes. The soles were heavy with mud and the leather scarred and furrowed like the faces of old men who've worked in the fields all their lives. He held them at the tips of his fingers and away from his precious nose. The man who wore them probably took them off in the heat to stick his toes into the moist, irrigated soil. A chorus of laughter went up when the guy held them high, then fell when he dropped them back to earth. He rummaged some more down the row until he found a sack three-quarters filled with chili peppers.

"Hey, I'm gonna keep these," he declared and dug his hands into the sack.

When everyone saw this they all began to clamor around for the other abandoned sacks. They claimed their right by how close their rows had been to the Mexicans beside them. The sacks belonging to the man working on the rows next to ours were lying, already sewn, on their sides. Nardo walked over and placed his hand on the first one. Two other guys came over and began to argue about whom the others belonged to, but my brother was stronger, and after some half-serious pushing and shoving they walked away grumbling.

"Look, Manny," he said excitedly, spearing up his shirt-sleeves. He lifted one sack by its ears and pounded it on the ground, packing the chilies down its belly.

"We got more here than it takes us two days to pick," he said. "Hey, you can even buy your baseball mitt."

I looked down at the sacks, then far out in the distance at the little clouds of dust still rising and disappearing where the vans had been pulling away. I wondered how long I would have had to work to fill those sacks, and my weariness stretched as wide as the horizon. I thought of the baseball glove, all clean and stiff and smelling of leather, and of myself in the cool green lawn of center field, like on the Bonneville Lakes golf course Nardo always talked about. I imagined I was already on the baseball team at school, and people were looking at me. Not these people picking chilies or those sent away in the vans, but people I had yet to know, looking at me as I stood mightily in center field.

RIDING UP
TO RUBY'S

Kim Stafford

Ruby was an old lady who lived up the canyon by herself, and her relatives hired me to do chores for a dollar an hour whenever I could get there. A dollar an hour made the math easy to figure, especially since my mom told me to always round down. "Round it off to the lowest amount," she said, "so they'll hire you again." I brought in Ruby's firewood, and I'd sweep, or sometimes I'd move things around where she told me to, and sometimes I'd just sit on that deep old couch of hers and listen.

She lived by herself, and she could cook and do most things, but she really didn't know what day it was, or even the year. Sometimes she called me by her grandson's name, Little Joseph, or by the name of one of her childhood friends. Sometimes she didn't seem to know I was there at all. But she talked all the time, like a canary I heard once, that just sang and hopped around its cage from sunrise to dark. All the time I was there, she was hardly ever still.

She was always fiddling with something, or knitting, or

doing this thing with a little hook on worn-out socks, or mending some old edge of a cloth with a silver needle and black thread. She never used thread to match, like my mom did, but always black so she could see it, I guess. And as she worked, and I worked, she talked about her old friends, saying their names, and telling things. Sometimes she talked about them to me, and sometimes she talked to me like I *was* them.

I almost forgot to tell you my name is Rob, and I'm an only child, and the only boy living in our whole canyon. But Ruby didn't call me Rob very often, because she was having her spells.

"Let's do make the garden fine," she said to me, even though it was winter and almost ready to snow. I was holding up the rug, getting ready to go shake it outside. "Rebecca," she said, putting her hand out toward me, "do let me plant the beans this time?"

"The beans?" I said. "Let me shake this rug first, can I?"

"Shake out that old feed sack," she said, "then let's get the garden in! We got to have the bean trellis high, if we want a wonder crop!"

It took me a while to catch on to the different times we were living in. She was back about as old as me, and I was trying to be more grown up than her. I guess it was part of my job to be the one that kept things sorted out. I didn't mind a girl's name now and then, because I figured out that Ruby didn't know any better, but it was kind of confusing sometimes. But it was interesting, too, because you had to figure out who she thought she was talking to, and then try to answer like that person would.

I shook the rug over the porch rail, and when I came back inside, I had a chill inside my shirt, and I spent a long time spreading out the rug so I could be by the stove and get warm. Once I got settled on the couch to look at the chore list, she was holding out her hand again.

"If you let me plant the beans," she said, looking into my eyes, "I'll let you hold my little guitar. I'll even let you play the strings." Then she stood up and started rummaging around the place for her little guitar, and I hoped she would find it, because I wanted to try playing it, but pretty soon she found something else, and that started another story. She was standing by the hall shelves, holding up some skinny brushes.

"The paint set! Margaret, get the paper and let's do cards! Margaret?"

"Yes?" I said. "Okay, just wait a minute." I brought her some paper from the table, but she just stared at me. "Joseph," she said, "you're not Margaret at all!" Then she got set up at the table, and turned to her painting, mostly drawing garden plans with little flowers around the edges, and forgot I was there. I decided that was okay. I just let her talk and she let me work.

Once I'd get her settled with what she wanted to do, I'd go find some job, like maybe stacking kindling by the wood stove, or checking the mouse traps under the kitchen shelf, but the mice always got away and the cheese was gone. One day I noticed the quilt draped over the rocking chair had been torn on a nail. I brought it to her, and showed her the place.

"Thank you, child," she said. And she went right into mending it. It was amazing she could do daily things by pure habit—like mending, or lighting the stove without burning down the house—even though she didn't know it was now. After a couple hours like this, I would tell Ruby I had to go, and then I'd get my bike from by her porch and ride down the canyon for home.

It was my idea, actually, to have this job with Ruby. I heard my parents talking after dinner one night when I was in the other room. Their voices got quiet, like they did when they talked alone. But I got quieter where I was, and once the fire crackling in the stove died down, I could hear them, every word. They'd talk about all the neighbors, just gossip. My dad pretended he didn't care about it, but my mom always knew so much that he couldn't resist asking her. They would talk about the store owners in town, and then about the bus driver who never had married, and then the junk dealer at the edge of town, and then they'd work their way up the canyon, family by family. They'd skip over us, of course, and then talk about the Harveys, and then Mr. Baxter and his wife, who had just moved in above us, and then Ruby, the last house up the road. Of course the road went on into the forest, but Ruby was the last of us before it was just wild.

That listening is how I found out that the store owners had money problems, same as us, and the bus driver had a girlfriend at the other end of his drive to Canada. And the junk man trained police dogs to keep kids out of his wrecked cars at night. Somebody kept sneaking in and taking stuff. And Mr. Harvey, sometimes he cut down trees outside the sale area, when he was logging on forest land, and pretended it was a mistake. But sometimes he did work for free, if he liked the people. And Mr. Baxter, the blind man between us and Ruby, one night my father told all about him. When they were moving in, his wife told my dad that Baxter went blind in the war, and the last thing he saw was a fire as big as the sky, and that's all he could remember. No matter how hard he tried, he couldn't get back past that picture into happy things.

It was confusing, all that talk. I tried to concentrate on my homework, but I couldn't. I tried a math problem, but it was just numbers. And when I tried history, it was just numbers again, dates and battles and stuff. But the stories my parents told, they were about us, us in the canyon.

"Ruby's getting on," my mother said one night, while I

was listening like that. I was doing the Egyptians at the kitchen table. "And it seems like her family will have to move her to the city," my mother said in the other room. "Such a shame."

"It happens," my father said.

"Her people are clear out to Coeur d'Alene," said my mom. "They don't get home like they did a few years back."

"So she ought to go to them," my dad said. "Coeur d'Alene's all right."

"But it's not home," my mother said. "It's okay, but it's not home for her. She's fine where she is, only she doesn't have anybody close to do little things. That's all it takes, a few chores, a little help to keep her steady. It's not that they can't pay, but she doesn't ask."

I listened close, because chores had been a topic around our house as long as I could remember. My own chore list kept getting longer. I had inside things, like keeping my room clean, and putting away my clothes after my mom washed them. And then I had outside jobs. I burned the trash in a big old oil drum, and split the kindling out of cedar that smelled sweet. I had to shovel wood chips into the mud hole where my dad parked his truck, if it got too deep. That's just for starters. With my dad on the road so much, plenty of his chores turned into mine. But chores aren't a job. They're different. They're just like being home.

Sitting at the dining table that night, with my homework all spread out, I stared at the timeline in my history book. It went for four thousand years on just one page, from some Egyptians to some wars. I stared out at the dark, and my chore list kind of got mixed up with the timeline, and suddenly I had a plan. I could work for Ruby by myself. I could work for Ruby, stay away from chores at home, get paid a little, and maybe save money for a new bike. With a new bike I could get to town on weekends without being all sweaty.

Those new ones would coast on the flat part, and even the ridge where the river turned wouldn't wear me out, because the new bikes had gears to make it easy.

Besides, I started to think it was a good thing to have a job, not just for money. When my dad got home from his long truck drives, he was really tired, but he was all kind of filled up, and we'd sit down and listen to what he had seen and what he had heard about. He never told about the wrecks he saw, because that would worry my mom. (Sometimes he told me, when we were out working in the barn.) But at the dinner table, he went on forever with his fork in his hand and his dinner cold on the plate about some buffalo he saw, right from the road down by Dixon, and that Indian battlefield at someplace called Wisdom, and the way purple and gold can roll out across the land at sunset where there aren't any mountains in the way, and this hundred-foot statue of a lady they had on the ridge over by Butte, with lights all over her you could see from town. Stuff like that, with sometimes a bite of steak stuck on his fork for ten minutes while he talked, before he put it in his mouth to chew. His job for money was driving, but his job for himself, seemed like, was seeing all those things and remembering what he wanted.

And it was the same for my mom. When she came back from the photo shop in town, she was just about exploding with news. Someone had complained once about his pictures being blurry. He drove clear into town to get them, because my mom called that the prints were ready, and then the whole roll was blurred. After that, my mom would open the packages to make sure the prints were clear before even calling the customers. So she knew everything about everyone—their vacations, their parties, funerals, weddings, their new babies, all that stuff. It seemed like only the mail lady knew more, from the postcards she read sometimes. It seemed like a job was the way you really found out about the world.

I went into the living room, and on the couch my parents both looked at me.

"Your homework done?" my dad said.

"Almost."

"Well?"

"I was wondering if I could do chores for Ruby," I said, "like it was a job." My parents looked at each other, then back at me.

"So," said my mom, "you've been listening to everything we said?"

"I just started thinking," I said, "because there was a place in the timeline where I got stuck, and so I was thinking, and I happened to hear the part about Ruby. Do you think that could be my job, all by myself?"

My dad looked at my mom. "Your call, babe," he said. And she looked up at me, like she used to think I was shorter and just then realized I wasn't. It was easy as that.

So right then I worked out a plan with my mom, and she called to share it with Ruby's daughter in Coeur d'Alene, and next thing I knew I had a letter from the daughter with the deal: a dollar an hour, and I got paid every month, forty dollars a month at the most, and see how it goes.

When I first went up to Ruby's, she was all dressed up in this old-fashioned, long dress, and sitting in her chair in the living room that was like a museum of junk. She had old rocks in glass boxes, and paintings on plywood boards hanging from the rafters, and also a painting of a garden on an old saw that you were afraid might fall off the wall and cut you, and clothes on hangers stuck on wall hooks, and bunches of dry plants tied up with string, and lots of other stuff. She had me sit down on the couch. We just sat there for a while. Then on the table I saw this list of chores her daughter had made up, and we had a talk about them, but it got real relaxed right away, and sort of confusing at the same time. Ruby started talking, I started working, and after that we just did what we thought of. I did everyting on the list the first day. Later, I started seeing other things Ruby needed that the daughter hadn't noticed. So I did them, too. And Ruby talked while I worked.

I nailed that board on the porch step with a hammer I found in the garage, so it wouldn't tip you over. And I pushed the pipes back together where icicles leaked out of the gutter from the roof. Then I rubbed soap on the bottoms of the kitchen drawers, so they didn't squeak and stick so bad when you needed a spoon or something. When I swept, I turned back the edges of the rug and got the old dirt along with the new dust. And I took all the books out of the bookshelf to put them in right side up, sort of looking at them as I went. They had all kinds of old photographs and poems and stuff stuck in between the pages. I always put them right back, after I read them. Ruby didn't mind if I took my time, because she had a lot of it.

At my house, nothing changed much. There was school, and sometimes I had friends over, when I could talk them into walking the mile up from the main road and walking back down when it was time to go. And of course I had my homework, and my own chores, too. But about every other day, right after school, I'd remember Ruby might have some work for me. No one ever had to remind me. I kept my own hours and dollars written on a postcard, and every four weeks I'd mail it to Ruby's daughter, and she'd send me some dollars in an envelope. I always rounded down, but sometimes she rounded up, so I did okay. I kept those dollars in a shoebox under my bed. I think I counted them so often, those dollars got as soft as Ruby's hands.

I would take my bike out from behind the garage, and

make sure the tires were pumped up, and put an apple in my pocket from our tree in the yard, if I could find one that wasn't rotten yet, and then I'd ride up the canyon. The road gets real twisty and dark, because the canyon is deep. You can always hear the creek rushing down below you. You have to be really careful and listen for cars, because it's hard to hear them over the sound of the creek, and the mail lady drives on the wrong side. But there aren't many cars at all, unless they might be some stranger trying to take a short cut through the mountains. They got stuck up there, and my dad or Mr. Harvey had to go pull them out. I'd be careful riding, because strangers go pretty speedy, as my dad said.

Sometimes on a Saturday morning the sun just comes down as far as the tops of the trees, making them gold. And if you ride too fast, your lungs get burned from the cold air. You mostly go through blue light, the shadows of the mountains. There was that bunch of houses and sheds where the Harveys lived, with their big logging truck parked by the barn. And then there was the meadow with the horses, where the canyon widened a little bit. Then the dark part with the spruce trees reaching out into the road. Then the place where you could get blackberries in the summer, the field nobody used. That was my favorite part. And halfway to Ruby's you come to Mr. Baxter the blind man's house, him and his wife.

Right before this really sharp corner there was their white house by itself in the trees. Behind the house, the mountain went up steep, and the place was crowded up against the road without hardly any yard at all. And the way the wind worked in the canyon, the snow drifts were always extra deep right in their front yard. The snow from the whole canyon would pile up there, when it drifted loose in the wind, and cover just about anything, even the front porch. But in the yard, right at the edge of the road, there was a clothesline, and sometimes Mrs. Baxter working at it. And there was this contraption out on the grass by the clothesline, like a little shed, only it didn't have walls. It sat on four little wheels and had an old tractor seat in the middle, and a steering wheel not exactly hooked up to anything, and then some kind of motor on a steel bed all covered with tar, and wires, and some lights tied with black tape to the frame. Mr. Baxter had been working on his machine for about six months, ever since they moved in. You never saw him in the yard, or even through a window. I guess he only came out at night, because he could work then just as well as any other time, and nobody would bother him. He didn't have a job, except to make his shed thing. My dad said he got disability, whatever that was. It didn't sound good, if you just worked at night on something crazy.

So every time I rode my bike up to Ruby's, there would be something new on the machine, but no sign of the blind man. I wanted to slow down and really study it, but I was afraid he would see me—I mean I was afraid he'd hear me slowing down—so I just kept pedaling, but I studied the machine as I went by to see what was new. Sometimes, if Mrs. Baxter was in the yard, I could stop and talk to her and look off sideways at the machine.

"Why, Rob, going up to Ruby's," she said once.

"Yes," I said. "Got my jobs today."

"I see you're looking at Jack's sculpture," she said. I asked her what that word was. "Sculpture," she said, "that's like art. He just makes what he wants to. Always has and always will, I guess." She was quiet, looking at me. There was a kind of light around her, because the sun came from behind.

"Is it true the last thing he saw was a sky full of fire?" I said.

"Who told you that?" she said. Her eyes closed part way.

"I don't remember," I said. "Is it true?"

"Hey," she said, "your dad told you." And she stuffed her clothes real fast into the basket and turned to go into the house. But halfway to the porch she turned around, with the big basket in her hands.

"Don't be afraid of him," she said. "He just does what he has to do."

Then I rode on into the dark shadows at the curve. I rode on feeling the blind man watching me. I rode along wondering if I was in trouble for saying the wrong thing, saying what my dad said. But I guess it was a secret at the Baxters, about the big flash in the sky. I wondered what Jack Baxter wanted to make with his sculpture, because it was different every time. But I didn't ask Mrs. Baxter any more. I just looked every time I went by. Sometimes when I rode up to Ruby's, it seemed like the farther up the canyon you went, the crazier things got. First Mr. Baxter, then Ruby, then some tourists with their tires spinning where they got stuck way up in the mountains. I heard how they could swear, when I went sometimes with my dad to help them.

Mr. Baxter's machine looked like it would get stuck for sure if you tried to drive it anywhere. One time there was a new row of fruit boxes nailed along one side. I couldn't see what was in them, except one had some levers coming out. Another time, there was some of that sparkle stuff they put on Christmas trees, like icicles, spread around under the wheels. One time there was a headlight out of a wrecked car, fastened onto a board and aimed straight up toward the sky, with red wires coming back to the pulleys the steering wheel went through. I wondered why a blind man needed a light, but there it was. And one time there was a whole row of bells, old horse bells, on a leather strap tied with baling wire to the top of an old TV screen. It was getting crowded like the inside of a car where people keep loading stuff and never unload. But it wasn't a car. It was a shed on wheels, with extras, mostly junk.

When the snow came, I had to wrap cord around my tires not to slip on the road, but I knew how to do it so I could still ride after the snowplow opened up the road. And when I went past, Mr. Baxter had shoveled the snow away from his sculpture, mostly throwing the snow out onto the road. Then the snowplow had come along just before morning, and pushed the snow all back into the yard. You could see where Mr. Baxter had tried to shovel the snow away again, with just little bites in the snowdrift where he had scooped at it. And it looked like he was making a place to drag the shed out to the road, like maybe he was going to move it on its wheels somewhere. He was keeping that place clear where most people would put a car, and where the snow got deep when it drifted.

But I mean mostly to tell you about Ruby, because that's where I was going. My job went on for months, me working and her talking, and her daughter sending the dollar bills. Some days Ruby talked and made me dizzy. But I kept sort of listening while I did something like cleaning the ashes out of the stove with the fire still burning. I had to concentrate, or I might roll a hot coal onto the rug. I got the ashes in a tin pail, and she talked while I swept ash into the dust pan, like I'd seen my mom do. It got so I watched my mom and dad a lot, when they worked around the house, so I could see better how to work at Ruby's, so she could talk all she wanted and I could still earn my dollars.

Then something bad happened. I remember it exactly. When it got to be about March, we had a really deep snow that drifted heavy, and some of the trees came down over the wires. We had to dig my dad's truck out, and I dug down to my bike and shook it off. It took everybody a few days to get things opened up, and then I rode up the canyon one morning, and what I saw I could hardly stand it. I had to just keep going. At Ruby's, Ruby was having one of her clear days. "Hello, Rob," she said when I knocked on the screen. "How's the day for gardening?" I was all hot from the road, but I didn't want to talk much.

"It's sunny," I said, "and the road's clear all the way, because the snowplow came today." It was Saturday, and I could stay as long as I wanted. The light was kind of skinny on Ruby's face. Then she turned around and sat down in her chair, and was just ready to start her talking. I took a deep breath. "The snowplow smashed Mr. Baxter's shed thing," I said.

"His shed?" said Ruby. "His garden shed." Inside my head, the look of all those wires and lights and wheels and work made me too sad.

"Do you have any chores for me?" I said. I didn't feel like talking about Mr. Baxter right then. It got smelly in Ruby's house, so I wanted to open the doors a few times, going in and out, maybe carrying wood or shoveling the walk.

She started talking, but I wasn't listening this time. I was thinking of Mr. Baxter finding all those broken boards with his hands, reaching down into the snow to find the pieces. I saw him crawling around in the dark, trying to know what had happened. Or maybe his wife told him, and she kept him from going out to the yard. Maybe they just held each other, like my mom and dad did sometimes, when there was something they didn't want to tell me. I felt like that myself, while Ruby was talking. Because Mr. Baxter, even if he was crazy, he had a job to make his sculpture, and now it was just all junk again.

When I saw the mail car out by Ruby's box, I opened the door and went down the walk. The driver always rested awhile at Ruby's, because that was the last house up the road. The mail lady would sit in her car and sort out letters and catalogs for the other boxes going down. She was always ready to talk, if she had time.

"Wouldn't you know it," she said, "that new snowplow driver took out half the mailboxes between here and town. I guess he couldn't see them in the drifts, but what a mess. Most folks had their boxes propped back somehow, so I could leave the mail. But I guess he hit that curve too fast and it's the end for old Baxter's time machine. Why'd he have to shove it out by the road like that, like it was a car? I guess the drifts kind of obscured it, and the driver didn't know what he was hitting. Smashed that time machine to smithereens."

"Time machine?" I said. "Was that a time machine?" I thought of the lights, the blind man's lights aimed at the sky. A machine for traveling back before the war and everything.

"He thought it was, the old coot. We've all watched it grow, and it's just kindling now." Suddenly I wanted to get back to Ruby. She might not be clear for long today, and I wanted to be with her.

"Is there anything for Ruby?" I said. The mail lady looked up at me, and shut off her engine. She liked to talk so much she always got to the place where she had to shut off her engine. It was suddenly real quiet in the whole canyon.

"I guess I won't be driving up this far next week," she said.

"Why not?" I said.

"On account of Ruby's being moved, of course," she said.

"Moved where?" I said.

"Rob, I'm sure your mom told you they decided to take her home." Then it was quiet again. The mail lady was looking at me.

"But she is home," I said.

"I know, but she's old. Her daughter wrote to stop delivery. No one told you?"

"No," I said, "I didn't know that." The mail lady looked

back down at her letters. Then she looked down the canyon.

"Why do *I* have to tell you this?" she said.

"When are they?" I said.

"Any day, I heard," said the mail lady. "It'll be hard for her to leave the place. You've made it good, Rob. You've made a difference. But when the power went out last week, I guess it scared her family. You can understand that."

"She was fine," I said. "I had plenty of wood stacked up inside, and she was fine." I felt my face getting hot, like I was the failure of the whole thing. Like Ruby had to go not because she was old, but because I didn't do enough work.

"I know she was fine," said the mail lady, "but time passes and things change. It had to happen eventually." Then she started her car, handed me a skinny catalog for Ruby, and turned her head away to back up and turn the car around. She was gone by the time I went inside.

"Anything for us?" Ruby said. "Lula, honey, anything they sent our way? I do want to get that seed catalog so we can pick out our beans. Kentucky Wonder or Blue Lake Bush. How shall we ever decide?"

She went on talking garden to Lula, her little sister, and I just sat there listening and studying her face like I had to memorize it. Inside her eyes, it was eighty years ago, and I was a child my own age, but different. To her, I was a sister, and then a cousin, and then a friend in the old days. I didn't know how to get back there and be with her.

"Mr. Baxter's time machine got all smashed," I said.

"The garden will be fine," said Ruby. I put my hand on the back of her hand, which was soft and warm.

"I said Mr. Baxter's time machine got all smashed," I said. "He can't go back before the war." Ruby looked into my eyes.

"You'll see," she said, "the garden will still be there, because you can plant it wherever you go." She was quiet for a while, and then her hand turned over and closed around mine. "Rob," she said, "you'll take care of my garden for me, when it's your turn." I just looked in her eyes. Her hand was warm.

"Yes," I said. Her old clock ticked awhile, and she held onto me.

"That's fine," she said, squeezing my hand. "You'll do it fine." And then she let me go. I got up, and she was quiet while I worked, for the first time ever. All the books were right side up, and the rug was clean. The kindling box was so full you couldn't fit another stick in. The refrigerator didn't have anything in it going rotten at all, and the dishes were organized on their shelves like a museum. I could see the black stitches around the red patch Ruby had fixed on the quilt over the rocking chair. After I had checked all around, we just sat and looked around. Then we looked at each other, and then I said goodbye, and she did, too.

"Joseph," she said, "you go easy down that canyon. Never know what you'll find around the bend."

When I rode my bike down the canyon it was just starting to get dark. My eyes always get funny in that blue light, especially with snow everywhere. There was that meadow where the lupine bloomed every summer. It was like I could see that blue color through the snow. It was all white, but there was a blue from summer, too. And around the corner, there was the beaver dam across the creek, and I felt like I could see every stick inside the dam, even though it was covered with ice and snow drifts. I started seeing everything I could remember. I saw the pine tree where the hawk nested, even though it got cut down last summer for firewood by the Harveys. When I came to the white house in its shadow place, I thought I saw Mr. Baxter's time machine, the whole thing with seat and lights and steering wheel, right there by the clothesline. When I came closer, I saw the splintery boards scattered around in the snow, too. But then I saw it standing up, like he'd made it. I had to just keep riding, because it was getting even darker. And around the corner, in the old field, I saw Ruby's garden, laid out in a little flat place in the snow. It was there by the creek, and it wasn't, and it was. I stopped my bike to look at it in the dark. The garden was there, with little mounds of beans and rows of shadows. My breath made steam all around my face. I had to stop breathing just to look hard. Maybe that's what it was like to be old, to see all those things at once and love them and want them and have them and not have them and want to tell someone, and when you were old, someone had to be there to listen.

The next day it was Saturday. I was sitting up in my room, and out the window I saw Ruby's daughter driving up the canyon in her big car. Mom said they had hired my dad to go up the next day with his truck, to pick up her stuff. But it was just the daughter now, going for Ruby. In about an hour, the car came back and stopped in front of our house. My folks went out to say goodbye, but I stayed upstairs, watching from back inside my room. Ruby and I had already had our goodbye, even though maybe she thought I was someone else. In the car, Ruby sat on her side, her hands folded in her lap. I couldn't see her head, but I could see her hands. She would remember me, maybe, with a girl's face and a cousin's name, but she would remember something of her own about our times together. And I would remember her.

By the time I finished thinking all these things, the car had driven away and the yard was empty. Looking out at that dirty snow, with the tire tracks curving into our place and then going away, I felt something climbing up through my body. It was a painful feeling inside my face, where I cried sometimes, but also inside my hands when I would work.

This thing inside got as big as my whole body. Bigger. I guess this thing I was feeling was my job now, my work, what I could do. I was a listener, and I remembered. And something would happen in my life because of that.

When it got to be summer, a few months after they took Ruby away, I hid my bike in some trees by the road, across from the field no one used, and I climbed up through the hills, up out of our canyon, all the way to the top. It took the whole morning to get there, but then I could see all over the world. There was the mountain they called Silver Shadow up north. I could see way up where our creek started. I could see the road like a little thread, like the creek was guiding it down out of the forest. I could see Ruby's house and where the road went and found Baxter's and then went around the bend where I couldn't see. That patch of smoke farther down, that was town, with the sawmill making everything blue. I could just see a glitter of windshields at the wrecked-car lot. And then I could see off to the west, where I would probably go when I got older, down the river to Coeur d'Alene, maybe, or clear on to Spokane, or even farther, places I didn't know the names of.

When I turned back and looked down the ridge to Ruby's house, it was like remembering. It was like I was older, and far away, but I could turn and see her place, and inside myself I could hear her voice. All her stories were inside me. I didn't want a new bicycle then, not even one with those gears. I wanted to do something that would keep me feeling like I did right then, looking down on the canyon where I started and wondering what I might be able to do, off there in the world, in that place I couldn't see.

LESSONS

Marilyn Sachs

It was the best job I ever had. Mr. Alexander paid me ten dollars an hour and always gave me a bag of pastries to take home.

"You don't eat enough," he told me. "If I was your father, I wouldn't let you look like you do, like a skeletine."

"Skeleton," I corrected. "And my father doesn't care what I look like or what I eat."

"Is it possible?" Mr. Alexander's round, rosy face turned severe. "If I had a daughter like you ..."

Mr. and Mrs. Alexander had three sons—all of them working in the business, and all of them as large and plump as their parents.

"You know, Charlotte." Mr. Alexander leaned his elbows on the bleached wood table in his kitchen. "I wanted a daughter. Even when I was ... was ... very short."

"No, no," I corrected. "You mean young or little."

"So?" Mr. Alexander questioned. "Short and little are the same. No?"

For the most part, all I had to do was come once a week for two hours and get Mr. Alexander to talk. Or read newspaper articles with him and discuss them. He didn't want any lessons in writing; his elder sons or their wives took care of letters.

"But to speak. To express myself. To let people know how I am thinking."

"Better to say, 'To let people know how I think, or what I think about.'"

At first, we met at the café in the mid-afternoon, before the dinner hour. But even then, there were phone calls and problems with sick waiters or delayed shipments of hazelnuts. Finally, Mrs. Alexander insisted. "You'll take an hour off a week, George. It won't kill you to be away for one hour and go home. The boys and I can look after everything. You know, Charlotte," she added, turning to me, "this man has no life out of the restaurant. He works seven days a week, and he's no youngster anymore."

"Stop already!" Mr. Alexander ordered.

"All his life," Mrs. Alexander continued, "he's worked like a horse. First, back in Greece, when he worked for his crazy uncle, like a slave, and then here."

"I had a family to support," said Mr. Alexander. "We had no money. We had nothing."

"Yes! Yes!" Mrs. Alexander waved a plump arm. "That was then. But now ... you know, Charlotte, every time I want to go away on a vacation, all he can think of is what will go wrong if he's away. And if by some miracle I get him to go away just for a weekend, he worries all the time!"

"Stop!"

"So when finally he tells me he wants to learn how to speak properly, I'm happy. Finally, there's something that doesn't have to do with the business. Something aside from the business."

"Enough! Enough!"

"So that's why I asked you, Charlotte. I always noticed you, and I always thought how smart and decent you looked. Not like most girls nowadays with all their makeup and tight clothes."

Mrs. Alexander had hired me one afternoon, when I was sitting in the back of the café, eating my weekly fix—a chocolate-raspberry eclair. It was just at the beginning of my senior year in high school, and I was reading Kafka's *Metamorphosis* for my honors English class.

"Excuse me, Miss, but I wondered if you might be looking for a job?"

Mrs. Alexander stood there, smiling, and smelling like mashed potatoes. Each of the Alexanders smelled like something good to eat—Mr. Alexander like one of his magnificent pastries, and the sons like whatever was the special of the day.

"Excuse me?"

"Oh—I'll explain." Mrs. Alexander plopped down into the chair opposite me. "It's to give lessons—English lessons—to my husband. Maybe once a week for two hours. You're an American girl, right?"

"Well, yes, I am, and . . . and . . . I could use some work, but I've never given English lessons before. I'm not sure I know how."

"It's just to talk to him," said Mrs. Alexander. "Once a week to talk to him and correct him. For a couple of hours. Maybe on a Wednesday or Thursday afternoon when we're not so busy. The rest of the time, he's in the kitchen cooking and baking, or he's talking Greek to me and the boys. He wants to talk better, not to sound like all those new foreigners who just came over."

Mrs. Alexander had the softest face, and her smile was kind. Now that my father and I had so little to do with each other, her smile almost disabled me. Hardly anybody—except occasionally for my honors English teacher—smiled at me like that.

"I could call your mother, if you like, and explain who we are. Maybe she could come in and meet us."

"Oh, no! I don't have a mother. She's dead, but my father and my stepmother both want me to work—more than I'm doing. As a matter of fact, I need to work more."

"Well, it would only be for a couple of hours. We could pay you—maybe ten dollars an hour. Would that be enough?"

Ten dollars an hour! Twenty dollars a week! Eighty dollars a month! Nearly twice as much as I was making baby-sitting. Enough to pay most of my school expenses and have enough left over for my weekly chocolate-raspberry eclair.

"Yes," I said. "Yes, that would be fine. When would you like me to start?"

From time to time, Mr. Alexander's youngest son, Paul, would let me in when I rang the doorbell. He was the only unmarried son, and still living at home.

"He goes to college at night," Mr. Alexander told me. "I wanted him to go full of the time, but ..."

"Full-time," I corrected.

"Yes, full-time, but he's too proud. He wants to pay his own way. I can afford it, Paul, I tell him. And his mother tells him, too. We want him to be a doctor or an engineer, but he's studying business administration. Why? I ask him. Why study business when you already work in a business? Study something ... something ... out of your hands."

"I think you mean—out of your experience. But Mr. Alexander, what would you study, if you could? I mean, if you were young again, and could go to college?"

"Young again? Ah, if I was young again." Mr. Alexander sat there smiling and nodding. Even inside the kitchen of his house with nothing cooking on the stove or baking in the oven, he still smelled of pastries.

"Art," he said, his cheeks flushing even redder than they already were. "Art. Like in the museums. Not like all those modern ugly things, but like they made in my country long ago. The statues—the beautiful statues—I would like to make statues. I would like to make them out of pieces of stone."

"Blocks of stone."

"Yes—I would make them beautiful—all those young boys and girls with their beautiful faces. I would make them—nothing ugly like what you see today. Ah, you're laughing at me, Charlotte."

"No, I'm not, Mr. Alexander. I'm just smiling because I'm thinking you already are an artist with all those fantastic eclairs and napoleons, and the wonderful cakes you make. Like the one you sent home with me that had a big yellow flower on it with a bright red heart."

"How about some tea, Charlotte, and a piece of my hazelnut torte? I brought some home for you."

"No, thank you, Mr. Alexander," I told him firmly. I felt he was paying too much for me to spend any time eating or drinking during his lesson. And besides, he always insisted on sending some of his cakes home with me anyway.

Another time he told me about his uncle. "Not a bad man. Maybe he had a temper, but he really wasn't a bad man. Don't listen to Melina. He taught me everything he knew, and if you think I bake good . . ."

"No—say, 'If you think I'm a good baker.'"

"Yes, you should have tasted his pastries. He used to make strudel that melted in your mouth. Mine is like lead compared to his. And his chocolate-rum-custard babka—ah, that was a work of art."

•

Lorna never ate any of Mr. Alexander's pastries, but my father did—along with me. Lorna was more interested in her figure.

"You don't know what you're missing, Lorna," my father said, shoveling another piece of the coconut custard napoleon into his mouth.

"It's really disgusting how the two of you eat," Lorna said. "At least Charlotte doesn't gain any weight, but you, Fred—lately, you're really looking like a tub of lard."

My father laid his fork down on his plate and looked sorrowfully at the remains of his cake.

"Anyway, Charlotte," Lorna continued, "I was wondering if Mr. Alexander would make me one of those phyllo chocolate cream cakes for my office. I know it's Don's favorite cake, and since I'm supposed to bring dessert for everybody at the Christmas potluck party, I guess I may as well bring that. I know he generally charges about fifty dollars for a sheet cake, but if you ask him, I'm sure he'd give you a break."

I put my fork down too. "No!" I told her. "I can't do that."

"Why not?" Lorna demanded. "Employers always give their employees breaks." She held out her skinny arm with the gold and jade bracelet on it. "Don gave me thirty percent off on this and my gold chains—practically at cost."

"I can't because he's paying me a lot for the lessons, and he always gives me cakes—free of charge—to take home."

"Now, Charlotte, I'm only saying you should ask him. Maybe you could just say you wonder what one of those sheet cakes would cost, and I just bet he'd give you a good price."

"No!" I said. "He's such a good, kind man. I just couldn't take advantage of him."

Lorna shook her head. "You're going to have to learn a few lessons yourself if you want to get along in the world. You just don't have any backbone. That's your trouble."

As usual, my father didn't say a word. He just continued looking at the uneaten piece of cake on his plate.

"When did your mother pass away?" Mr. Alexander asked gently.

"Four years ago," I told him.

"It's terrible for a child—especially a girl, I think—to lose a mother."

Most of the time now, I hardly remembered her. But sitting there in Mr. Alexander's warm, quiet kitchen, I remembered. Before the sickness, when she used to sing to me before I went to bed. She used to sing one of the Beatles' songs—"Octopus's Garden"—and I could suddenly almost hear her voice and smell her warm mother smell as she bent over me.

"She was sick for a long time, and she suffered a lot," I finally said.

"And your father?"

"We used to be very close, especially after my mother died. He said he was going to be both mother and father to me, but then he married Lorna, and he changed. I hate her."

"No, no, don't hate. Very bad to hate."

"Didn't you ever hate, Mr. Alexander? Didn't you ever hate your uncle? Tell the truth."

"Yes, I did," Mr. Alexander admitted, "And maybe some others, too, but I always felt sorry later."

Mr. Alexander talked eagerly during the lessons, and his speech improved. I told him to try to speak English with other people besides me, and he said he felt shy with other people. He felt they laughed at him, but with me he didn't have to worry. Sometimes he wanted to listen. He was interested in everything that was happening to me. He was interested in my family, in my boyfriends (none), my grades in school (mostly A's), my dreams of being a writer one day.

He had to listen very hard because sometimes I became so wound up, I spoke too quickly, and he would ask me to repeat myself. He sat there across the table from me, leaning forward, his round face tight in concentration.

"So," he said, "you'll go to college when you graduate? Where will you go?"

"I'd like to get away and go to one of the eastern colleges like Yale or Harvard. My advisor thinks I could get in, but Lorna and my father now, too, say I should go to city college or state and live at home. They say they can't afford to pay for me at an out-of-state college. Not even if I get a scholarship."

"Maybe they don't want you to go away from them. Maybe they love you so much they would miss you if you went away. My older boys stayed home until they got married."

"No," I said. "No, they don't love me, and nowadays most young people go away to college. I want to go away. They just don't want to spend any money on me."

"I suffered so when my sons left home to get married. Even more than Melina. I cried all the time."

"That's because you're such a wonderful father," I told him. "I wish you were my father."

Mr. Alexander had tears in his eyes. "I would miss you too, Charlotte, if you went away."

"Well, it doesn't look as if I will."

"Maybe we could make another lesson."

"Arrange another lesson."

"Yes, if you could, maybe Monday afternoon and Thursday."

"Oh, I'd love to. And I do think, Mr. Alexander, that you are really improving. You seem to have a lot more confidence when you speak, and you're not making so many mistakes."

"That's because I have such a good teacher," Mr. Alexander insisted.

•

"Extra lessons?" Lorna said. "Well, that's fine. Maybe you should ask him for a raise—say fifteen dollars an hour."

"Absolutely not," I told her. "He's paying me a lot, and I'm not going to take advantage of him."

Lorna shrugged. "Most language teachers probably get twenty-five or thirty dollars an hour, so he's really taking advantage of you."

"Lorna, I'm not a real teacher. I'm only a high school kid."

"That doesn't matter. Anyway, he seems like a nice man, and he certainly thinks a lot of you."

I sat up straight in my chair. "How do you know? You never met him."

"Well, I happened to have a few hours off today, so I thought I'd just stop by and say hello. Very nice man—very friendly and obliging. What is the matter with you, Charlotte?"

I must have known what had happened because I was already staring at her with fury. "What did you say to him?"

"Oh, we talked abut this and that—his kids and you, and then, you know, Charlotte, like I said, I just mentioned that I wanted to order that phyllo chocolate cream cake for my Christmas party. I didn't even ask him what it cost. I just said I supposed it would be expensive, but right away he said he'd make it for me for free. I guess he thought you would be coming to the party, too, but you don't have to tell him you're not."

"I hate you!" I yelled, springing up. "I hate you! I hate you! I hate you!"

"Did you hear that?" Lorna said to my father, who had continued eating.

"You spoil everything. You make everything dirty."

"Fred, are you going to let her talk to me like that? She's a spoiled brat, and it's your fault."

"Charlotte," my father said in his wimpy voice, "come on, Charlotte. It's not so terrible. Charlotte!"

But I pushed my plate hard, and hurried away from the table. "I hate the two of you," I shouted back at them.

All I could think about that whole weekend was how I could explain to Mr. Alexander that I had nothing to do with Lorna's request. I thought about our lessons and how much they meant to me. I thought about the quiet kitchen where each of us could speak freely, and how Lorna was trying to muddy the waters. But I wouldn't let her. I would tell Mr. Alexander not to make her the cake or, if he did, to charge her the full price. And I would let him know that I wasn't going to be at the party. My face burned with humiliation. What must he think of me? I couldn't wait for the next lesson.

But there never was another lesson.

"In his sleep," Mrs. Alexander said. "He went to sleep, and he never woke up. But Charlotte, the lessons made him happy. I only wish he could have started earlier. I only wish . . ." But she was too overwhelmed to continue, and all I could do was cry with her. I couldn't explain about Lorna.

"They're closing the café for a week," Lorna said, shaking her head. "Poor man! Of course, he was much too heavy. Fred, you'd better watch yourself or you'll end up the same way." She reached over and patted my hand. "What a shame for you, Charlotte! A kid like you isn't going to find another job like that in a hurry. Anyway, they'll be open the week before Christmas so I'll still be able to pick up my cake. That's what one of the sons told me. I guess he'll be doing the baking now."

"I don't want you to!" I shouted at Lorna.

"Charlotte, what is the matter with you?"

"I don't want you to! I don't want you to take advantage

of him! I won't stand for it! I won't!" I jumped up and stood over her, my fists clenched and the tears exploding all over my face.

"Fred, you'd better make her stop. She has some nerve talking to me like that. Who does she think she is?"

"Lorna," said my father, "let it go!"

"What?"

"Let it go!" My father stood up, and put an arm around me. "Now you calm down, Charlotte," he said. "Just calm down. Everything is going to be okay."

For the next few weeks, I avoided Lorna. I couldn't look at her, much less speak to her, and I know she avoided me. I mourned for Mr. Alexander, and I suffered, thinking he had died without knowing the truth about me. Every morning when I woke up, the pain quickly rose into my throat and stayed there all day. I thought it would never go away.

I was also afraid that Lorna would still try to wangle the cake out of Mrs. Alexander in spite of what my father told her. I waited for that to happen. I didn't know what I would do, but I waited. She ended up buying a chocolate cake from the local baker for her Christmas party. After that, the pain began lifting.

My father came with me to Mr. Alexander's funeral, and sometimes, later on, he even stuck up for me when Lorna and I quarreled. Not most of the time but enough so I knew he was still there for me when I really needed him. Mr. Alexander's son wasn't as good a baker as his father, but I kept going back anyway once a week for the chocolate-raspberry eclair, and for Mrs. Alexander's smile. After a while, I found another job at a video store that paid me five dollars an hour.

THE PILL FACTORY

Anne Mazer

I took the freight elevator to the seventh floor of the pill factory. Even though it wasn't yet 8:00 A.M., it was hot and the air smelled stale, with a faint medicinal overlay. One or two people drifted like bits of dust through the huge warehouse.

I found the lunch room where workers met before the start of the day, sat down at a scratched Formica table, and looked around. There was a coffee pot on a shelf, a small refrigerator, and some jackets on hooks. A battered romance novel lay face-down on the table. The single greasy window looked out on other brick warehouses painted with the faded names of long-gone companies.

"Well, well, our summer worker." A massive woman in denim overalls and a black T-shirt came into the room, carrying an open box of danishes, frosted doughnuts, and crullers in one hand, and an umbrella in the other.

"Hello," I said.

The woman plopped down on a chair, dropped the umbrella on the floor, grabbed a doughnut, and devoured half of it in one bite. Shiny red jelly oozed over the side of the doughnut and dripped onto the table.

"Want one?" Her stiff, oily hair was combed straight back. She shoved the pastry box in my direction.

"Oh, no, thanks."

"Go on, take one. You need the energy around here." Her eyes narrowed as she looked at me.

I pulled out a cruller. It was my first day. I didn't want to make a bad impression.

"You look twelve." A fine spray of doughnut crumbs flew out of her mouth as she spoke.

"I'm sixteen."

"No, you're not." She poured herself a cup of black coffee and dumped six packages of sugar into it. "Tastes like mud," she grunted. She leaned toward me, breathing heavily. "What's your name?"

"Meredith." I wanted to know her name, too, but was too shy to ask.

"Meredith, have you ever worked before?"

Did baby-sitting qualify? Did mowing the lawn or raking leaves? I was trying to think of an answer that would sound adult and respectable, when suddenly she looked up. "You're late again, Polly."

"No, I'm not, Barbara." Polly grinned crookedly. Her two front teeth were missing, and she had a black eye. I tried not to stare. "Are you the summer girl?" she asked.

I nodded.

Polly yanked a stained apron down from a wall hook, then fastened it around her dumplinglike body. Her hair was thin and brown, teased into a feathery pouf. "What did you come to this place for?"

"Money," I said, then blushed at my answer.

"That's the only reason to be here." Polly winked at me out of her good eye.

"Leave her alone," Barbara said. "Don't get her started with your bad attitude. And I told you. You're supposed to get here early."

"Oh, sure." Polly slid into the chair next to me and gave me a friendly poke in the ribs. "I love to work."

I had two older brothers in college; I had to work. There weren't a lot of jobs around for kids my age with no experience, and this one paid more than most. I was lucky to get it.

Barbara studied me. "We'll put her on the glue machine, don't you think?"

It had an ominous sound. I imagined something sticky, vile, poisonous. Myself stuck to a machine, unable to escape.

"Sure, sure," Polly said, winking again. "It won't be too hard for her."

"Blaaatttt!" A bell rang insistently.

With the back of her fist, Barbara wiped the crumbs from her face. Her lips compressed into a thin line. "Punch-in time, girls!" she ordered. "Punch in!"

Next to me, Polly's hand snaked toward the pastry box, disappeared inside, and snatched a danish. With a quick, furtive motion, she shoved it into her apron pocket and rushed out the door.

Barbara pushed me after her. Right outside the lunch-room was a time clock. She pulled a yellow card from a gray metal slot. "Write your name," she ordered. "Then punch in like this."

"Blaatt!" As I slid the card into place, the machine beeped angrily.

"Cooome on!" Barbara bellowed, balling her fists on her massive hips. "Time to work!"

Suddenly Polly dashed back into the lunch room.

Barbara breathed loudly through her mouth. Her face was red from chin to forehead. Hidden in the large, slablike cheeks were two gleaming, shrewd eyes. "Po-ol-*ly!*"

Polly darted back like a mouse flushed out of a hole. As she passed me, she pinched my arm and cackled. "Got the last drop of coffee," she whispered. "She couldn't stop me."

I had never been in a factory before. I expected hundreds of workers sitting at small tables and an unearthly din of machines, but there were only a few scattered in the vast space of the warehouse. Eleven people, Barbara told me when I asked her how many worked here.

She hurried me toward a rickety wooden table in the middle of the floor. A short distance away were rows and rows of high metal shelves stacked with boxes. Across from them, a stooped man stood at a narrow table and wound strips of sticky packing tape around a box. A single bare bulb burned above his head. In another corner of the warehouse were three machines with huge plastic funnels. A woman wearing green clothes and a mask over her nose like a hospital nurse turned the crank on one of them and pills clattered into an amber-colored bottle placed directly below the mouth of the funnel.

"Here," Barbara grunted. She indicated an old wooden chair in front of the rickety table, and lowered herself into the chair opposite. She pointed a huge red finger like a sausage at me. "I'm only going to say things once. This is the glue machine."

It was a small, unprepossessing thing, barely a foot long and only eight or ten inches wide, with a couple of rollers on each end and a wide belt that reminded me of flypaper stretched between them. Barbara flicked on the switch, and the belt began to turn with a slow monotonous hum.

"Now it's on. You got that?"

I nodded.

"Now. See this? A vitamin bottle. Understand?"

"Of course," I said, a bit impatiently. Maybe I had never

had a job before, but I could recognize a vitamin bottle when I saw one.

She laid it in front of her and took a label from a stack at the side of the table.

"A label. For the bottle. Watch carefully." Her enormous fingers were surprisingly nimble as she fed the label face-up through the rollers, then snatched it by the edges as it came out the other end.

She held it up. With a deft motion, she centered the label, pressed it down on the bottle, and smoothed the edges. "See that?"

"Sure."

"Nothing crooked, nothing sloppy. And no air bubbles! You got it?"

"Uh-huh."

Standing up, Barbara kicked her chair back and slapped a label in front of me. "Then do it."

I picked up the label, inserted it between the rollers, watched the belt coat it with sticky glue, and grabbed it as it came out on the other end. Then I carefully stretched it over the glass bottle and smoothed it out from the middle toward the edges.

"There," I said, pleased I had done so well the first time.

Barbara frowned. "See that air bubble there? You'll have to do better than that."

I grabbed another label and put it through the machine. It tore as I pressed it over the bottle.

Silently Barbara handed me another label.

This time, the label slipped as I pressed it down. It ended up slanted on the bottle.

"If you can't do any better than that, don't bother coming back tomorrow."

I gritted my teeth and began again. The factory paid twice as much as baby-sitting, and I was sick of having milk spat in my face, of playing endless games of cards, of washing dishes and folding and ironing other people's laundry. And besides, I wanted to be out in the world, to prove that I was as smart and capable as the rest of my family, that I wasn't the baby anymore.

It wouldn't be easy to find another job either; I had put in thirty applications before I got offered this one.

I slid the label into the machine, retrieved it, and stretched it tight over the bottle. It didn't wrinkle, slide, or tear. "Yes!" I said triumphantly, holding up the neatly labeled bottle.

"Okay, you did one," Barbara grunted. She nodded in an almost friendly way. "Now do a thousand more."

At first, I worked slowly: ten labels in three minutes. Then I picked up speed: fifteen labels in four minutes, then twenty in three. Every now and then I glanced at the large industrial clock mounted on the wall opposite. After two hours, I had several boxes of neatly stacked and labeled vitamin bottles.

"Blaaattt!" The bell rang again, bone-shattering and fierce. In spite of myself, I leaped from my chair. Then I forced myself back and picked up another label.

"What are you doing?" It was Polly, her hands and face covered with fine yellow dust. "It's break time!"

"Barbara told me to finish these."

"Are you crazy?" Polly reached over and switched off the machine. "You have to stop now."

"But ..."

She gripped my arm with clawlike fingers and yanked me to my feet with surprising strength.

"It's okay," I explained. "I don't mind. I'm not tired."

Polly clucked in dismay. "Bad idea. You got to take your break." She pointed to the lunchroom. "Tomorrow you'll be running there."

I shook my head no.

Polly grinned, showing the gap in her teeth. "You'll see."

In the lunchroom, Barbara sat at the table, her massive legs splayed in front of her. She was breathing heavily through her mouth. The box of pastries was almost empty. "You're late," she said to me.

"I was finishing my work."

She snorted with contempt. "You only get fifteen minutes, by law, and if you miss it, it's your tough luck."

Next to me Polly cackled and pinched me hard, as if to say I told you so.

"Did you bring something to eat on break?" she asked. "No? I'll share mine with you." She reached into her apron pocket and pulled out the danish that I had seen her grab earlier. Only now like her hands and face, it was coated with yellow dust.

"Here." She thrust half of it into my hand.

I looked down at it.

"Go on," Polly urged me. "I don't need it. You can have it."

"I'm not really hungry."

Barbara snorted again. "That's vitamin dust, girl. It won't hurt you; it'll make you healthy."

I nibbled at the edges of it.

"Isn't it good?" Polly said.

"Mmm." It was good. I took a larger bite, then went over to my backpack and pulled out a book. The two women stared at me.

"Oh, a smart girl." Barbara ran her fingers through her stiff, oily hair. "One of those."

"I knew she was," Polly said. "I knew it the minute I saw her."

I tried to concentrate on the words on the page, but they jumped around like insects. I could feel Barbara and Polly's gaze on me. I turned the pages and pretended to read while the large black and white clock above us ticked steadily; I imagined that its sound rose above the clattering din of the factory and overwhelmed it.

By the time the lunch bell rang two hours later, I had filled a dozen more boxes with labeled vitamin bottles: Best Rite, Serv You, American Vites, Health Kaps. They were cheap, inexpensively made vitamins, intended for local drugstore and supermarket generic brands, and their labels had bars of red, white, and blue on them, implying that it was not only healthy but patriotic to take your vitamins. I imagined vitamins making their way into my body, leaving indelible streams of color, then washing into my brain.

I was a gluer; I worked the glue machine. Those were the words that kept going through my head as I labeled vitamin C, multi-vitamins, and B complex. I had a good-paying job for the summer, and I was determined to succeed. My family would be proud of me. I was a baby no more.

A man came and hauled the labeled bottles over to Polly and another woman, who were filling them. Then they were capped, sealed, and taken away.

Just before the bell rang, Barbara came over to check on my progress. She was accompanied by a man I hadn't seen before. He was dressed up more than the other workers, in slacks, a white shirt, and a tie.

"This is the summer girl," Barbara's eyes narrowed as she looked down at me. "You can see her work."

"Not bad," the man said in a soft, nervous voice. He was tall and graying and blinked rapidly as he looked at me and my work.

"The manager, Mr. Kredler," Barbara announced.

"Nice to meet you," I said.

Barbara scowled at me. "She's one of those smart girls. How long do you think she'll last?"

I held my breath. Would I get thrown out before the day

was even done? I needed the money. Money meant college. College meant I could choose what I wanted to be: lawyer, scientist, or teacher. But first I had to make it through this summer.

"Oh, she'll do," Mr. Kredler said mildly. He nodded at me as he turned away. "She'll do nicely."

We had half an hour for lunch. It was hot in the lunchroom. I rolled up my sleeves and ate a peanut butter and jelly sandwich and an apple and drank a carton of juice. Barbara didn't show up, and Polly ate a meat stew. Another woman came in silently, took a brown paper bag off a shelf, and left. I opened my book and read a few pages. Next to me, Polly rolled up her sleeves and pulled out a nail file from her purse. Then she dug out a mirror and a comb and teased up her hair. When the bell rang, she gave me another friendly dig in the ribs. "Don't work too hard, kid, huh?"

"Okay," I agreed.

She winked at me out of her good eye.

Break time again. It was two hours and many, many labels later. It was almost unbearably hot now. I drank three cups of water in the lunchroom, washed my hands and face, and wished I hadn't worn corduroy pants to work. Barbara sat at the table, drinking can after can of soda. Her eyes were thin, glittering slits between heat-swollen lids. Sweat dripped down her reddened face. Polly stripped off a long-sleeved shirt. She was wearing a light T-shirt underneath, one that revealed a tattoo of a rose on her plump, pale arm.

Blaaaattt! Before I could read even two pages, the bell rang again. I closed my book and stumbled to my chair.

Mechanically, I thrust label after label through the glue machine. My stiffened fingers worked in an automatic rhythm. I had a numbing feeling of unreality, as if I would never leave this factory, would never stop the endless round of bottles and labels.

At 4:45 P.M. I stood up and wiped my forehead with the bottom of my shirt. How was I going to get through the next fifteen minutes, much less the next ten weeks?

That evening, I wheeled my bicycle down the ramp. My hands were raw, my shoulders ached, my head was spinning. My fingertips crackled with glue. I stumbled out into the world, taking deep breaths of the hot, smoggy air.

The next morning I was up early. My parents and older brothers had already left for work; the house was cool and silent. I took my bagel onto the patio and sat looking down at the garden, at the long sparkling trail of grass, and the roses bordering its edges. At 7:30 A.M. I wheeled my bike out of the garage and rode past the neat, orderly houses, down to the boulevard. Already there was a lot of traffic on the street.

I pedaled past gracious old houses with wide lawns, then past rapidly deteriorating neighborhoods and shabby storefronts, and into the decaying heart of downtown. At 7:55 I was riding up in the freight elevator with my bike. The doors opened. There were the shelves of jars waiting to be filled, and vats of pills that perfumed the air with their sharp, medicinal smell. I wheeled my bike onto the factory floor and left it standing in an empty corner.

The bell rang. "Punch in, smart girl!" Barbara hollered.

Another day in the pill factory.

And another and another. The hum of the glue machine spoke to me. It said, "I have a job, I have a job." Or did the job have me? I wasn't sure any more. I lived by the bell. It was mounted near a greasy window, a huge bell, the size of a gong, and ushered us from one world to the next. Its furious bleat penetrated to the dustiest, most distant corner of the factory. The sound reverberated through my bones, muscles, and blood, drove all thoughts out of my mind, and let me know that I was part of a machine, that I was only as good as the labels I pasted. When I heard it, I jumped up like an automaton and rushed to my station or abandoned it.

"I can't stand it!" I said to my parents after the second week. I pushed my hair away from my face with a sweaty hand. Tears came into my eyes.

"It's only for the summer," my father said. "Don't quit; it's not good for your self-respect. Finish what you start."

Then he reminded me that my grandmother had gone to work in a factory at age six; my grandfather had worked every day of his life driving a truck, flipping burgers at a hot grill, or doing manual labor; and both my parents had earned every cent of their college education. My brothers worked part-time during the year and all summer long. "Work or die" was the family motto.

My mother shot a reproachful look at my father. "If it's too hard for her, she can quit."

Did she think I couldn't handle it? Did she think I was too young, too immature, too weak? Too much of a baby? I sat up straighter and brushed away the tears. "I guess I can give it another try."

In the factory, the sunlight beat through the dirt-smeared windows, and the temperature kept rising through the long afternoons. There was no air-conditioning. The air was gritty, almost a palpable force in the room, pressing against me. Rivers of sweat ran down my face and back. I sipped at glasses of water and tried to position myself in front of the floor fan, which sent a timid, ineffectual breeze down the center of my table. My shoulders ached, my fingers were stiff, my mind was dazed by the clattering of the machines, the whirring of the fans, the ticking of the clocks that were everywhere. I worked in a big box that trapped hot air inside it, a noisy box with splintered wooden floors and large windows that didn't open. It was stifling, suffocating, maddening.

But I could do it. At least for now. I could push myself a little farther every day.

After the first day, I had lost my name. "Summer girl," Mr. Kredler called me, during his rare appearances on the floor.

"Smart girl!" Barbara saluted me, her small eyes glittering as she inspected the boxes of labeled bottles.

"Hey, kid," Polly whispered, passing me half of a pastry and a dig in the ribs or a pinch on the arm to go along with it.

I answered to all of them and didn't mind that they seemed to have forgotten my name. After all, didn't Mr. Kredler often have a smile and a compliment for my work? Didn't Barbara sometimes offer a begrudging word of praise? Didn't Polly help me find supplies and show me a shortcut or two?

"Where's your book?" Barbara demanded.

"Left it at home." I unpacked my lunch bag: the usual sandwich, apple, and juice.

"Want some goulash?" Polly offered. "I made it last night." She waved her steaming fork in front of my face.

"It smells good," I said, but I couldn't stand to eat anything hot in eighty-eight-degree weather.

Barbara continued to watch me. "How come you didn't bring your book?"

"I didn't feel like it." Each day, I had been able to concentrate less and less on the words on the page. After working alone on the machine for hours, I wanted talk—any kind of talk. And human companionship. "It was boring," I added.

Barbara stared at me suspiciously for a moment, then

slapped her knee with an enormous hand and burst out laughing.

I smiled back at her.

"Sure you don't want any goulash?" Polly said again.

I shook my head.

"Want to see a picture of my boyfriend?" She pulled a wallet out of her pocket and rifled through the plastic flaps. "There he is," she said, showing me a picture of a pale scowling man with his arms folded across his chest.

"And here I am." She showed me another picture. She wore a black lace nightgown and was smiling with her lips pressed tightly together. There was a faint dark circle around one eye.

Polly snapped the wallet shut and stood up. "Anyone want a soda? I'm going downstairs to the machine."

Barbara tossed a few quarters across the table. "Get me a root beer."

I finished my sandwich and drank my juice. Looking out the window, Barbara slurped the remaining soda in her cup. Then she turned to me.

"Don't be like her," she said. "Or me." She wiped her forehead with a crumpled napkin. "I wanted to go to school once. I like horses. I wanted to be a veterinarian."

I imagined those massive hands smoothing the flanks of a horse, carrying buckets of feed, administering medicine.

"Why didn't you?" I asked.

"Not everyone's a smart girl like you. Don't argue with me!" She glared at me. "Wet behind the ears! Do your job, save your money, then get out of here. Don't come back."

A few days later, Violet came to work on the glue machine.

"Show her everything," Barbara ordered. "You're going to train her."

Violet sat down on the chair across from me and folded

her hands in front of her. Her gray hair was in a bun, she was wearing a flowered dress with a high frill around the neck, and she looked as though she were going to a Sunday school picnic, not to a factory.

"Have you ever worked a glue machine before?" I asked Violet.

"This is my first job," she quavered.

"There's nothing to it," I said several hours later for the hundredth time. "You can do it."

Violet pulled the label off the bottle with trembling hands. "I'm not much good at anything," she whispered.

I sighed. "It just takes practice. Don't give up."

"Thank you, Meredith," she said humbly.

She fumbled with the pile of labels, then slowly tried to insert one into the machine.

"The other way," I said quickly. She had glued quite a few on the wrong side.

"Oh, dear!" She stared at the label a moment, as if trying to figure out what it was for.

"Put it in the machine," I reminded her.

Her hands shook as she put the label through, then centered it over the bottle.

"Is this good enough, Meredith?"

The label wasn't straight and there was a large air pocket at the side. "Do it over," I said. As she watched me, I thrust another label into the machine, pressed it down hard over the bottle, and then, without stopping, did another and another and another. I felt like a star athlete showing off my moves.

Violet's pale eyes filled with tears. "I'm not suited for any kind of work."

"You'll be fine," I said. I took a breath. "You're doing a good job. It just takes time."

"Thank you, Meredith. You're so very kind."

•

I expected her to be fired by the end of the week, but Violet stayed on. She worked with almost painful slowness, filling less than half the boxes that I did. But no one seemed to notice, except me. I wondered if she was related to the owner in some way. How ever had she gotten the job? I couldn't even imagine her filling out an application form.

It was strange. Polly and I discussed it, wondering why she had never worked before. I wondered if she had a family, though somehow I knew the answer to that, and not just from her bare, ringless hands. Day after day, she wore her old-fashioned dresses with their frilly white collars. In spite of the heat, she always wore stockings and narrow lace-up shoes. She ate her lunch by herself; if anyone spoke to her, she raised watery, red-rimmed eyes, and answered in a tremulous whisper. Barbara mostly ignored her. Mr. Kredler didn't know she existed. And Polly, who had been so kind to me, was impatient with her.

"Get it yourself!" she snapped when Violet asked her to take down a box of empty bottles. Or, "That's none of my business," when Violet spilled vitamins all over the floor and went to her for help.

When Violet continued to put her time card in upside down, Polly cried, "How can anyone be so dumb!"

Violet stared at her. Then she burst into deep wrenching sobs. I had never heard an adult cry that way and I was terrified. My heart was pounding, I couldn't breathe right. I grabbed the time card from Violet's hand and punched it in.

"It's okay, it's okay," I said. "Everything's all right, Violet. I fixed it."

She raised her mottled, tear-streaked face. "Thank you, Meredith. You're so very kind."

"It's nothing," I muttered. I handed her a tissue. "Really, it's nothing."

•

From then on, Violet turned to me for everything.

"Meredith, can you help me? Meredith, what should I do? The label is ripped. Meredith, is it all right if I get a drink of water?"

Suddenly I was the person in the know. And I liked it. I wasn't the baby anymore. I felt tough, almost as tough as Barbara. But little by little, Violet began to get on my nerves. For one thing, her repetition of my name began to wear me down.

"Meredith," she cried all day long. "Meredith, I can't do this. Meredith . . ."

"Don't call me that," I snapped one hot afternoon. It was pure irrationality; what else was she supposed to call me?

Her eyes filled with tears. "I'm sorry, Meredith."

I took a deep breath and spoke slowly. "It's all right. You're fine. You're doing fine."

"I'm no good," she whispered. "I'm just no good."

"Don't say that!"

"You're so very kind, Meredith."

I didn't know whether to laugh, cry, or scream.

She looked down at her hands. "Meredith, is it all right if I go to the little girl's room?"

I began to hide from her. At lunch time, instead of eating with Barbara and Polly, with Violet sitting a few feet away, I crept to the back of the warehouse, where the long rows of metal shelves ended and where there were stacks of boxes thrown haphazardly on top of each other. There I sat on the floor and read until the bell called me back.

"Where were you, Meredith?" Violet asked me timidly as we sat at our table, labeling bottles.

"I needed some quiet."

"Oh." Her lip trembled. "Am I too noisy for you?"

Once again, I found myself reassuring her. "It's not you, Violet. You're all right."

One day I came back from lunch and found her sitting at the table, pale and unmoving.

"Violet?"

She didn't answer me.

"What is it?" I asked. "What's wrong?"

Violet hid her face in her hands and rocked slowly from side to side.

Then I understood. "They fired you, didn't they?"

She raised her head to look at me. "No," she said. "I quit."

I stared at her in shocked silence. My mouth opened as if to speak, then closed.

She looked at me calmly. "I don't like it here."

Violet left a few minutes later. "Thank you, Meredith," she said in her quiet voice. "You were so kind."

She picked up her purse and adjusted the lace collar of her dress. Then she walked to the elevator and pressed the button. She did not look at the clock. She did not punch her time card. She did not glance at Barbara, who was unloading boxes of pills from a ramp, or at Polly, who stared at her briefly, then went back to filling glass bottles. She didn't even look back at me.

I imagined her going back to a single room in a building where no one knew her. I imagined her making herself tea, sitting very straight in a hard wooden chair. I imagined her making the rounds of stores, factories, and agencies, looking for another comfortless job.

It came to me, with the force of a blow, that she was brave.

Suddenly I wanted to be just like her, to say, "I quit!" to

Barbara, to forget about the time clock and the bell and the glue machine. I wanted to ride the freight elevator down to the ground floor and take my bike out into traffic. And then I would ride and ride until I had left the city entirely behind me, until my eyes were blinded by sweat and my muscles shook from exhaustion. Then I would throw myself down in the long fragrant grass of some quiet meadow and spend the rest of the day on my back, staring at the sky, only the sky.

But I stayed. Day after day I rode my bike through the city traffic, cursing drivers and pedestrians, slamming on my brakes, and pedaling harder than I needed. Week after week I picked up my paycheck and put it in the bank. And each time I punched my card into the machine was a triumph of will, of persistence, of strength. I had a job. I could do it. I was proud. I was tough. I was a gluer on the glue machine.

FORTY BUCKS

Graham Salisbury

Shane, a tenth-grader at Farrington, and Jimmy, a seventeen-year-old Kaimuki high school dropout, were just about to lock up the Taco Bell on Kalanimoku Street when the old man came in.

This old guy wasn't old like a one-soft-taco-and-low-fat-milk kind of old, but more like a two-bean-burritos-with-no-onions-and-ice-tea old guy. Tired little bulges like tiny hammocks hung under his eyes, and above, at a slight angle, he wore a brand-new black felt cowboy hat with a gray feather hat band.

"Mister, we wen' close already," Shane called from behind the counter. Jimmy was in the back mopping the floor.

The old man smiled and nodded and went on over to sit at a table as if Shane had said, "Come on in and have a seat."

"Hey, mister, I said . . . tst."

Shane frowned and shook his head and walked out around the counter to look into the night to see if anyone else was hanging around out there. When he saw no one—no cars, no nothing—he started to go over and lock the door but decided not to because he still had to get the old man out of there.

Shane went to where the man had set himself down and, resting his hands on the table, leaned forward and gently said, "Mister . . . we wen' shut down already. You gotta go. We're closed."

The old man scratched his slightly whiskery chin and thought a moment. *"Una cerveza fria, gracias. Solo una cerveza fria."*

Shane looked dumbly at the man, then straightened up. "Hey, Jimmy," he called. "Try come."

Jimmy came out carrying the mop. "What? Who's that? We're closed."

"I know that, but he don't. You tell him."

Jimmy leaned on his mop and said, "We closed, old man. No food."

The old man yawned, rubbed the back of his neck, and said, *"Que cerveza tienes? No, olvidelo. No importa. Deme lo que tenga frio."*

"What'd he say?" Jimmy asked.

Shane shrugged. Wasn't Japanese. Wasn't Chinese or Filipino. But it did sort of sound like Mrs. Medeiros when she got mad. "Maybe it's Portuguese," Shane said.

"Portuguese? You know Portuguese?"

"No."

Jimmy frowned. "How about sign language? You know that?"

"Only the sign on the door that says closed at eleven p.m."

"So what we going do?"

Shane and Jimmy stood there a moment studying the man, who sat there smiling up at them. *"Hay algun problema?"* the man said.

"Maybe he wants a burrito."

"Well, then he'd say burrito, wouldn't he?"

Jimmy shrugged and said, "We couldn't make him one, anyways, without turning everything back on again. And I ain't doing that."

The old man reached into his shirt pocket and pulled out a wad of crisp, clean twenty-dollar bills. He peeled one off and put it on the table. *"Es suficiente?"* he said.

"Put that away," Shane said. "We ain't selling anything. We're closed."

When the old man just looked blank-eyed at him, Shane added, "No likey talk, no likey money. Closed, *pau,* time for go home already."

The man frowned and peeled off another twenty-dollar bill and put it on top of the one already on the table. *"Basta con esto? Cuanto cuesta una cerveza?"*

"Hoo, the guy rich," Jimmy said. "For forty bucks I'll make him a Burrito Triple Supreme."

Shane scowled at Jimmy.

"Okay, okay," Jimmy said. "Just joking."

Headlights from a pickup truck pulling into the parking lot blared in the window. The driver gunned the engine, then shut it down. The lights went off.

"Aw, man," Jimmy said. "Now we got more people coming in. Did you lock the door?"

"No. I was waiting to get this old guy out."

Two boys about eighteen years old got out of the truck and shouldered their way through the door into the Taco Bell. One was kind of fat and the other tall and lanky with a tattoo of a knife with dripping blood just above his elbow. The two boys glared at Shane and Jimmy. The bloody-knife one noticed the forty bucks on the table and said, "You buying, old man?"

The old man smiled up at him. *"Estos no me entiende.*

Habla Español? Les puede decir que solo quiero una cerveza?"
Then he made drinking motions with his hand.

When the old man said *Español,* Shane knew he was
speaking Spanish because he'd heard his older brother say
that over and over last year when his brother was taking
Spanish in the eleventh grade. "Hablo Español, amigo," he
said about fifty thousand times. No, "*Yo* hablo Español,
amigo."

"Cerveza?" the old man said again.

The tattoo boy looked at his friend, then at Shane and
Jimmy. "The fock he say?"

Jimmy said, quickly, "Nothing. Who can understand
him? Anyways, we're closed."

The tall boy said, "Door's open, so you're open, and
we're hungry."

"If you don't believe me, look at the sign on the door,"
Shane said. "We closed fifteen minutes already."

The old man, looking as if he'd decided that he wasn't
going to be understood and was wasting his time by hanging
around, shook his head and got up to leave.

The fat boy glanced at him when he stood up, then
turned back and got in Shane's face, so close Shane could
smell his sour breath.

Shane took a step back.

The fat boy pulled out a long switchblade and flicked it
open and grinned when Shane turned nearly as white as a
boiled octopus.

When the old man saw the knife, his eyes squinted
down so slightly you almost didn't notice any movement in
them at all. Slowly, he sat back down, his eyes pinned on the
knife. He put the two twenty-dollar bills back on the table as
if he'd changed his mind about leaving.

The fat boy poked Shane's chest with his finger. "My
fren said Taco Bell is open, know what I'm saying?"

Shane nodded. "Yeah, but . . ."

"You like me stick you wit' this, or wot?"

Shane clammed up.

"*Eh, eh, eh,*" the old man said to the fat boy. "*No se ponga asi. Tranquilicese. Les invito a una cerveza.*"

"What'choo talking? German, or what?" the fat boy said, folding the blade back into the handle and putting the knife into his pocket. "Hey, Jojo, this guy talking German."

"Not German, you stupit. That's Russian," the tattoo boy, Jojo, said.

"Russian? No kidding? How come got Russian fut in Taco Bell?"

"Shaddup, who cares. Hey, you two. Make us some food."

Jimmy hurried back over to the counter and started to turn everything back on.

The fat boy swept his hand over the table, grabbing up the old man's forty dollars. "I could use this," he said, slouching over toward Jojo. The old man followed him with his eyes.

"What'choo looking?" Jojo said, glaring at the old man.

The old man kept staring, didn't even blink.

"Shet," Jojo mumbled after trying to stare the old man down and losing. He and the fat boy went over to a booth near the front window and slumped down into it and started mumbling about something or other.

Shane eased back around the counter to help Jimmy. "Maybe we should call the police," he whispered.

No, just make some tacos or something. If we call the police, these guys will come back again . . . and then we going *had* it."

Shane nodded. Maybe Jimmy was right.

Together they brought out some trays of cheese and refried beans and sliced lettuce and tomatoes and hamburger meat.

"What'choo like eat?" Jimmy called out to the two boys.

"Six tacos and six Burrito Supremes," the guy named Jojo said.

"And two root beers," the fat guy added. "Big Gulps."

"Big Gulp is Seven-Eleven," Jimmy said. "Anyways, we don't have root beer."

"Hey! I said I like root beer, and no make smart mout' or you going be sorry, you stupit taco flipper." The fat guy laughed at what he thought was a pretty clever insult, taco flipper.

Jimmy whispered to Shane, "How we gonna get root beer?"

"How should I know? Maybe go across the street to Foodland. You got any money?"

"Two dollars, about."

"Get some more from the cash register, then," Shane said.

"What if when I open it that guy comes over and takes the money like he took that old man's money?"

Shane thought about that, then searched his own pockets. "Here, I got another dollar. Just get three dollars' worth of root beer and get back over here as fast as you can."

When Jimmy started for the door Jojo looked up. "Hey! Where you t'ink you going?"

"Get some root beer."

Jojo laughed. "Hey, Wayne. He going get you some root beer."

The fat guy, Wayne, chuckled and slapped his knee. "You walk out that door, taco flipper, and you going meet Mr. Blade." He laughed some more and patted his pocket where Mr. Blade waited.

Jimmy inched back behind the counter.

Just then the old man got up and walked over to the table where Jojo and Wayne sat. He sat down next to Wayne, the guy who had taken his forty dollars. *"Creo que empiezo a comprender. Sois un par de golfos. Y estais molestando a estos jovenes."*

"Get out of here, you stupit Russian fut," Wayne said, scowling at the old man. He slid farther away, closer to the window.

"Devolverme el dinero y marcharos en paz."

"Where the fock you t'ink you are? Speak English."

Jojo was grinning, as if he were enjoying seeing Wayne squirm. "He's telling you how handsome you are, Wayne. I think he likes you." Jojo whooped and Wayne gave him a stink scowl.

"What's that old guy telling them?" Jimmy whispered, he and Shane watching from behind the counter.

"I don't know," Shane said. "But I can tell you this: he's nuts. Those two will cut him up and eat him alive. We gotta call the police."

Jimmy nodded and inched over toward the phone. One step, two.

"What you punks doing back there?" Jojo called. "Where's the food?"

"Coming right up," Jimmy said, leaping away from the phone.

The old man sat staring at Wayne, which made Wayne squirm even more. "Get off this seat, futhead, before I crack and pop you."

The man put his hand out, open, waiting for his forty dollars.

"I think he like that money back." Jojo said.

"Shh," Wayne spat. "That's mines now."

The old man waited, still staring.

Wayne snapped and whipped the back of his hand at the old man's face.

Quick as a lizard's tongue, the old man grabbed Wayne's

fist and held it in a viselike grip. Wayne grimaced, his eyes wild.

Shane and Jimmy froze, their mouths gaping open.

Jojo laughed, holding his stomach and sliding down in his seat.

"Como digo, lo mejor es que os marchais," the old man said calmly. *"Pero primero devolverme el dinero."*

Wayne struggled, trying to pull his hand away, but the old man held on. Wayne couldn't break loose. His face grew red, his eyes burning with menace. "You *had* it, old man. I going drag your bones out of here tonight."

"Come on, Wayne," Jojo said. "That's only one old gramps. You no can take 'um, or wot?"

Wayne reached toward the old man with his free hand, but the man twisted the wrist he was gripping and Wayne's head fell to the table. "Ow, shet. Let go! Let go! I going *kill* you! Ow, ow! Let go!"

"Call Mrs. Medeiros," Jimmy whispered frantically. "Ask her what we should do. *Quick!*"

Shane hurried over to the phone, took it off the hook, and hid down behind the counter. He dialed Mrs. Medeiros, who owned the Taco Bell on Kalanimoku Street. The phone rang and rang. Five times, six.

She answered on the seventh ring. "What?" she said, half-awake.

"Mrs. Medeiros, this is Shane. We got a problem."

"What problem? What time is it? Where are you?"

"I'm here. Taco Bell. It's eleven-thirty."

"What's the problem?"

"This old guy came in, but then these other two guys came in, and they're starting to fight. What do we do?"

"Call the police, use your brain. That's why I made you assistant manager. I'll be right down. You call the police." She hung up.

"She said call the police," Shane whispered to Jimmy, who didn't know whether to listen to Shane or watch the fight or make tacos and burritos or run for it.

Wayne yelped in pain and Shane peeked up over the counter. The old man was still sitting there with Wayne's head mashed down onto the table.

Jojo slid out of the booth and stood up, his bloody knife tattoo stabbing out like trouble. He didn't seem to know what to do. He glanced over at Shane and Jimmy and saw Shane still holding the phone. "Who you calling? Put that down. *Now!*"

Shane dropped the receiver. It broke when it hit the tile floor. Part of it bounced around on the end of the cord.

Jojo looked back at Wayne, then scowled when outside he saw a police car's blue lights flashing behind a Corvette stopped in front of Taco Bell. Two cops were getting out to give some speeder a ticket. "Shet," Jojo mumbled. "Hurry it up! Gimme the food."

Shane and Jimmy went to work, faster even than they ever did when the place was crushed with customers. In seconds they had the six Burrito Supremes and six tacos wrapped up in paper and in a sack. They slide the sack out onto the counter, keeping the counter between them and Jojo, who rushed toward them with pinched and angry eyes. "Where's the root beer?" he said.

"We ... we ..." Jimmy stuttered.

"Shuddup! Gimme some cups."

Shane pointed to the pop dispenser.

Jojo grabbed two large paper cups and filled them with ice that shot down noisily. "Wayne, let's go!" he said, filling the cups with Coke. He put lids on them and grabbed two straws.

Wayne all this time jerked around, still trying to get free, still with his head mashed down onto the table because the old man was twisting his arm so hard. Outside, the cops were making the Corvette driver stand spread-eagled against his car.

"Come on!" Jojo shouted to Wayne. "Stop fooling around."

But Wayne couldn't break free.

Jojo looked at the police, then back at Wayne, then hurried out alone. He fired up his truck and drove slowly out of there with the six Burrito Supremes and six tacos and two large Cokes.

Shane ran over and locked the door.

The old man smiled when he saw Shane do that, and he let Wayne the fat boy go.

Wayne sprang up and leaped over the table and jumped out of the booth on the other side. He stood facing the old man, rubbing his wrist. His small chicken eyes darted around, searching for Jojo, but there was only Shane, Jimmy, and the old man. Slowly he backed away, then turned and ran for the door.

But it was locked now. And you needed a key to get out.

"Unlock this door!" he yelled, banging on it with his fists, then slamming against it with his shoulder.

Shane and Jimmy didn't move. The old man kept smiling.

Wayne whipped out Mr. Blade and flipped him open. "I said open the door, you deaf or what?"

"Hijo, creo que es mejor que me devuelvas el dinero," the old man said.

"Shuddup! I don't speak Russian, you stupit." Wayne started toward the old man with his knife but stopped when another set of headlights flashed into the parking lot.

"Criminy, where are all these people coming from?" Jimmy mumbled.

"It's Mrs. Medeiros," Shane whispered.

Seeing the car pull up and also seeing the police lights, Wayne ran toward Shane and Jimmy, looking for a back door.

But the old man stepped in his way and grabbed his shirt as he ran by. *"Dinero,"* he said. *"Dolares."*

Wayne spat in his face.

Boom! Wayne was on the floor, one arm twisted up behind him and the old man's knee jabbing into the small of his back. Wayne winced in pain. "I'm gonna *kill . . . ahhh!"*

Jimmy gaped, not believing the old man could do what he was doing. Shane saw Mrs. Medeiros at the door, fumbling in her purse for her keys. He jumped up and over the counter and hurried to unlock the door.

Wayne thrashed and gasped on the floor.

The old man, tired now of playing around, twisted the knife out of Wayne's hand and kicked it under the counter. Then he reached into Wayne's pocket and took back his forty dollars and let Wayne go.

Wayne stumbled to his feet and took a swing at the old man but missed by a mile.

Shane had the door open now, and Mrs. Medeiros yelled, "Hold it! Stay where you are!"

But Wayne ran out the back, shoving Jimmy back against the refried bean tray as he ran by.

"Aw, *man,"* Jimmy said, pulling his hand out of the gooey muck.

"You!" Mrs. Medeiros called to the old man. "What'choo in here making trouble for? Shane, how come the police out there an' not inside here? What's going on around here?"

"It was those guys, not this old man," Shane said. "It was the other guys."

"What other guys? I only saw one."

"There was one more."

The old man pushed up the brim of his hat with his finger. *"Muchachos, ahora si que necesito esa cerveza,"* he said.

Mrs. Medeiros scowled at him. Then to Shane and

Jimmy she said, "You boys get to work and close this place down," and Shane and Jimmy did as she said.

She went over and sat at a table and motioned for the old man to sit down across from her, which he did. *"Pero que quiere?"* she asked him in his language.

The old man smiled, broad and full. He took off his hat and covered his heart with it. *"Señora, yo solo queria una cerveza, eso es todo. Solamente una cerveza."*

Mrs. Medeiros studied him a moment. Then she, too, smiled and the two of them went on in the foreign language that Shane and Jimmy could not understand while they swashed and clanked around behind the counter.

"Shane, Jimmy," Mrs. Medeiros called. "I'll be right back. Let this old man sit here while I'm gone." She got up and headed for the door with her keys jingling.

Outside, the cops were easing the handcuffed Corvette driver into the back seat of the police car. Mrs. Medeiros walked out just as they drove away with him.

"I gotta get a better job," Jimmy mumbled.

"Why?"

"Why? This place is too dangerous, man. Too crazy."

"Not. Here we got entertainment."

"Yeah, but one of these days some crazy going come in here and freak out and somebody going really get hurt and I don't want it to be me."

"Ain't going be you. Why somebody going hurt you? You and me, we nothing to anyone who comes in here. We're just like the pop machine or the garbage can. They don't see us. We just workers, part of the machinery. Crazy guys want more glory than us."

Jimmy looked at Shane, then shook his head. "You more crazy than the crazies, you know?"

Shane laughed and looked up as Mrs. Medeiros came back in carrying two bottles of beer. She took them over to the table and handed one to the old man, and the two of them talked and laughed and drank beer together like a couple of old friends from way back.

After a while, Mrs. Medeiros called to Jimmy, "Try bring me one paper and envelope from the office."

Jimmy got them and brought them out. Mrs. Medeiros pointed to the old man with her chin and Jimmy put the paper and envelope down in front of him. Mrs. Medeiros dug a pen out of her purse.

While the old man wrote something on the paper, Mrs. Medeiros said to Jimmy, "This man is from Spain. He's staying at the Waikiki Beachcomber. He said he was dragged here by his son and daughter-in-law as a retirement gift, when what he really wanted was just to stay home and work in his garden. But his son always thinks he knows what's best." Mrs. Medeiros chuckled to herself. "Sounds like my husband . . . anyway, all this man wanted was a beer."

Jimmy said, "But Taco Bell don't sell no beer."

"Well, duh, Jimmy," Mrs. Medeiros said, then shook her head. "This is why you should have stayed in school. Your mind needs more exercise."

Jimmy looked down at his hands, and Mrs. Medeiros added, "He thought this place looked like a cantina."

"It looks like the Alamo," Jimmy said.

Mrs. Medeiros studied him a long moment, then with a sigh said, "Why don't you just go finish up so we can all go home to bed."

The old man finished his beer and got up to leave. He whispered something to Mrs. Medeiros and handed her the envelope.

"Buenas noches, muchachos," the old man said, tipping his hat and heading toward the front door with Mrs. Medeiros. *"Que os valla bien."* He chuckled and vanished into the night.

"Weird," Jimmy said.

Shane agreed, "Weird, but pretty cool, yeah? The way he shame that punk, Wayne."

"Yeah, that was awesome."

Mrs. Medeiros handed Shane the envelope. "This is for you two," she said. "Lock up this time, okay? I'm going home already. This business going put me in an early grave."

Mrs. Medeiros left and Shane and Jimmy studied the envelope.

"What does it say on the front?" Jimmy asked.

"Para mis valientes amigos," Shane read slowly, stumbling over the strange words.

"What's that mean?"

"I only recognize *amigos,* which means friends, I think."

"In Russian?"

"Not Russian, you idiot. Spanish. All this time you thought that was Russian?"

Jimmy shrugged. "That's what those punks said."

"Sheese."

"Open the envelope," Jimmy said, and Shane tore the end off.

Inside, Shane found the two twenty-dollar bills and a note that he read slowly. *"El mundo necesita mas muchachos trabajadores como vosotros. Os ruego que acepteis este dinero."* And it was signed, *"Vuestro amigo, Manuel Rodriguez Martin, comisario de policia (retirado), Valladolid, España."*

"You understand any of it?" Jimmy asked.

"Well, I heard *muchachos* before, that means boys, I think. And there's *amigo* again."

"He gave us this money?" Jimmy asked.

"Looks like it."

"Hoo, maybe I'll keep this job after all."

"See, I told you. We're just part of the machinery. This is

like a tip, like oil for the engine that runs the place, know what I mean?"

"No, but what we going do when those two punks Jojo and Wayne come back? We better hide then."

"They not going bother us."

"How come you say that?"

"Because, number one, Wayne's going be piss off at Jojo for run out on him, and number two, we never went rat on 'um."

"What'choo mean, *rat?*"

"I mean we didn't call the police. We handled it ourselves."

"That's because the phone broke."

"So? They don't know that."

Jimmy thought about that a second, then said, "Yeah, you right. No police!"

"Of course I'm right. That's why I'm assistant manager and you the taco flipper. Come on, let's get out of here. How's about we unload some of this cash. You hungry?"

"Yeah. Where you like go?"

"McDonald's."

"Right on."

THE AVALON BALLROOM

Ann Hood

I'm only seventeen years old and already I work something like ten jobs. My only real job is at the Baskin-Robbins on Sixth Avenue near Thirteenth Street, scooping ice cream to NYU kids who don't need to work and an occasional famous person, like Jamie Lee Curtis or the guy who played Grandpa on the old *Munsters* show. My mother always tells me how Baskin-Robbins used to be more timely. Like once, when Nixon was almost kicked out of office, she said they had a flavor called Im-peach-mint. She thinks this is the funniest thing. My other jobs are just little odds and ends types of things—feeding people's spoiled pets while they're out of town or watering exotic plants.

The only job I can't do anymore is sell junk on the sidewalk, in the East Village near Astor Place where street people have a kind of flea market. One day I tried to sell some of my mother's old stuff. It basically just sits around the apartment or in her closet, but she came running down there like a crazy woman. She scooped everything up in her arms and started to cry. "Lily," she said, "how could you sink so low?" After that, she hardly talked to me for almost a week.

I feel bad that I did that, but I was mad, too. She knows why I "sunk so low." I need to come up with two thousand dollars so that I can go to Princeton in the fall. That's why I work all these stupid jobs and why I never get to go to the clubs with everyone else. I'm saving every penny to go to Princeton. Don't ask me why, but going there is like the most important thing in my life.

My mother only works at a bookstore, so she can't help me too much. We already buy banged-up fruit for half price at the Korean deli on our corner and day-old bakery bread to save money. My mother likes to say that we're resourceful, like it's an adventure the two of us are on. But lately I find myself wondering why she can't just get a better job. A real job. Why didn't she become a nurse or something useful?

As a last resort I might go uptown and ask my grandmother Pearl, my father's mother, for help. But I haven't even told her I've been accepted yet. I want to wait until I get more money together first. I hardly ever talk to her, and when I do, I hate to ask her for anything. Once, when I was a kid, I wanted a bike so badly I made the mistake of asking her. The one I wanted was navy blue, an English bike. Pearl said if my mother weren't so frivolous, I'd have a bike and a good pair of shoes and a decent haircut.

A few months later my mother shows up with a third-hand bicycle, kind of beat-up, plus we had to share it, but still. That's what she's like. So for now, I'll just keep scooping ice cream and feeding schizo Siamese cats.

Today, Tamara wants to eat lunch at Dojo. She says the chicken yakatori there is great. "We can split it," she tells me. "It's big enough to share."

Tamara is my best friend, and she knows that I never have enough money to eat in restaurants. Even cheap ones.

"It comes with a salad," she adds.

We're standing at Astor Place, looking at old magazines that a Rastafarian has spread out on the sidewalk to sell. He is also selling half-finished crossword puzzles from the Sunday *Times* for a quarter each. I focus on one, pretending to study it. All the clues that are filled in end in "biosis." I think that even with all my jobs, if I save every cent I earn, it will be over a year before I have that two thousand dollars.

Tamara is waiting for my answer. She picks up an old *Artnews* with an article about Andy Warhol in it. Her parents are psychiatrists—all four of them. Her mother and step-father live in this huge loft in SoHo, the coolest part of the city. And they collect art. Just in the living room alone they have a painting by Roy Lichtenstein that looks like a comic strip with a blond woman saying, "That's the way—it should have begun! But it's hopeless!" And they have an Andy Warhol Marilyn that Tamara's mother talks to sometimes. She says, "What do you think, Marilyn?" In the print Marilyn's all weird colors—green and pink and yellow.

Tamara sighs—she thinks Andy Warhol was a big fake—but I think the sigh is for me.

"I don't like Dojo," I tell her, although I do.

"I can pay," Tamara says without looking at me.

But I just shake my head. "Anyway," I tell her, "I have to feed this cockatoo at Bleecker Court before I go to work."

Tamara flips through an old copy of *Elle*. "You know," she says, "you *could* ask your grandmother."

I start to walk away. I have an impulse to run, fast, but I control myself.

"Lily!" she calls to me. "Come on."

Tamara is going to Berkeley in the fall. Practically for free. By using her father's address in Redwood City she can claim she's a resident of California. I imagine that Redwood City has streets lined with giant sequoias, air that smells of cedar.

"Or you could come to Berkeley with me," she's saying. She is holding the magazine loosely, so the pages flap like tiny flags. I stand on the corner and watch her. "I mean," she continues, now that she has my attention, "you don't have to go to Princeton just because your father did. I mean, you said he even dropped out."

"That's not why," I say, but softly so she doesn't really hear me.

"You could go to Berkeley," she says again. "Didn't your parents meet there or something? So isn't that practically the same thing?"

They met on Highway 1, each hitchhiking alone from San Francisco to points south. That's what my mother says, points south.

"If you come in later, I'll give you a free cone," I say. I wave goodbye to Tamara casually. None of this matters.

My parents were flower children. They looked like Sonny and Cher. When I tell my mother this, she frowns. "Lily," she says, "your father was somebody special. Nothing at all like Sonny Bono." Even when I try to explain to her that Sonny Bono is special in his own way, her frown remains, deepens. "He's the mayor of Palm Springs," I tell her. "He was married to Cher. Doesn't that count for something?"

Although I'd never tell my mother this, I've always found it both ironic and fitting that he was killed delivering flowers. Hit by a bakery truck on Houston Street at dawn, never even knowing he was going to be a father. Just riding his bicycle west, toward Sixth Avenue, his mind filled with thoughts of world peace and brotherly love.

To me, he's a stranger. But in our tiny fourth-floor walk-up on Thompson Street, my father is a myth, a hero, a god. Some days I almost expect to come home from school and find a shrine to him erected in the living room—candles burning beneath the Sonny and Cher photograph of him and my mother, his authentic World War II flight jacket carefully displayed, his old Avalon Ballroom poster for Big Brother and the Holding Company hung just so, and my mother kneeling in front of it all, worshipping the only things that he left us. My mother tells me how the flowers were thrown for blocks, how it seemed that somehow it had rained flowers. She says this often.

At night, when we both get home from work, my mother and I always share gifts. I bring old ice cream, discontinued flavors or a quart container filled with all of the day's leftovers. She brings paperback books with the covers ripped off, books that the store where she works is going to throw out anyway. Books like *What To Do If Your Teenager Joins a Cult*. We eat the ice cream and look at the books before we go to bed. The books are usually weird ones and the ice cream always tastes gritty, but she still looks forward to this time of night. She tells me that she loves the sour-milk smell on my hands. It reminds her, she says, of when I was a baby. "Babies always smell like sour milk," she says. Then her eyes get all teary and she looks off into the distance and I know that she's thinking. She's remembering how that bicycle just snapped in half like a toy.

　　My mother is very big on rituals. And our nightly one is just the kind she says that she used to have with my father. He used to bring home half-dead flowers and arrange them in empty bottles while she read him poetry. My father's favorite poets were Williams and Shakespeare and Ginsberg. "And me," my mother likes to say.

　　Tonight I am not into this ritual. Tamara came into the store with five other kids, all on their way to CBGB to hear The Tornado, a new band. "We'll wait for you," she said, but I had to feed the cockatoo and water about a hundred African violets for this woman who lives all the way over in the West

Village. So when my mother comes home all smiles under this bright blue beret she always wears, I ignore her.

There is really no place to hide in our apartment, but if there were, I would be there. Instead, I pretend that I'm doing my calculus homework and that she can't see me sitting there in plain sight on my bed, which is really just the couch opened up. Since she doesn't know yet that I'm ignoring her, she starts to tell me a story about a woman who came into the bookstore and ordered seventeen copies of a Shelley Winters autobiography. "Can you imagine?" she says when she's finished. "Hello?" my mother says. "Anyone home?" I print the number seven seven times, the number eight eight times. "Lily?" she calls from the kitchen. "Where's the ice cream?"

For an instant I feel guilty. We had a whole container of her favorite flavor, Rocky Road, left over and I didn't bring it home. She's standing at the foot of my bed and I look up, right at her, and say, "I forgot." Then, very seriously, I write the number nine nine times. I am solving an important mathematical problem.

The next morning, Sunday, I wake up to the sound of my mother typing at the kitchen table. She always spends Sunday mornings before she goes to the bookstore working on her poems. When she gets home at five, her hands are inky gray from handling *New York Times*es all day. Most Sundays I make her coffee in the morning and dinner when she comes home, but this morning I stay in bed with the pillow over my head while she works on rhyme and meter.

I'm thinking, why doesn't she write something that makes money? Maddie Hazelton's mother writes articles for magazines and gets at least two thousand dollars every time. I even tried to write one, but I got a rejection letter that basically said, "Forget it." My mother could do it, though. One article and my problem would be solved. One article about cellulite and I'd be on my way to Princeton.

Thinking about all this makes me feel more desperate than ever. So as soon as the door shuts I am out of bed and dressed. Before I leave I grab a handful of coverless books from the book box. When this box gets full, we lug it over to the library on Sixth Avenue or up to Mount Sinai Hospital and donate all of these books to charity. Charity, my mother believes, brings peace to the soul. She likes to tell me how on their one Thanksgiving together she and my father ran a food drive for indigent families. How, even at Princeton, my father participated in fund-raisers for leukemia, animal protection, starving children.

The book box is pretty empty considering we just made a drop two weeks ago, but still I choose the ones I am taking carefully. These are not books to be read by strangers or sick people. These books are gifts.

My grandmother Pearl's apartment looks like a set from a Woody Allen movie. It's large with high ceilings and lots of bookshelves. From the parlor windows the Hudson River is visible, a gray sparkling worm.

I don't go up there very often. Just Christmas when I bring her a prewrapped gift of talcum and cologne, in some floral French scent that Pearl has worn forever. I eat Christmas dinner with Pearl and Ottie, another old lady who lives alone in her building, too. They always serve food I don't like, leg of lamb or tenderloin of beef, all dry and overcooked until it tastes like sand. I'm always allowed to have one glass of wine with dinner and a cup of coffee afterward with vanilla Florentine cookies. Before I head back downtown, Pearl gives me presents. They're always practical things, like scarves or gloves or an umbrella. They're always store-wrapped, too, from Saks. Then I kiss her cheek, which is as dry and rough as the meat we had for dinner, and start to go home where my mother is waiting for me.

Pearl already has a shrine to my father. It's in his old bedroom, which still smells vaguely of a gym locker, all socks and soap. This shrine seems to be to an entirely different person, one who is crew-cutted and uniformed, who clutches his football helmet in an old picture in which he crouches, number 16, with the Princeton junior varsity football team of 1968. The clothes in the closet are V-neck sweaters, pressed chinos, frayed shirts with buttondown collars. The books are lined up alphabetically. A bottle of English Leather sits on the bureau, all the cologne inside long ago evaporated. In a drawer there is a class ring, unused tennis balls, a black and orange Princeton tie.

Every Christmas, when I put my coat on to leave, Pearl unlocks this door and lets me in. She whispers his name, Trip, as if not to disturb him when we enter. She tells me, softly, how he gained eight hundred yards in just one season at Princeton. She tells me that for her birthday that last year—her fiftieth—he sent her fifty white roses. "He forgot to bring one for luck," she always adds. I believe she thinks that somehow changed their luck, his forgetting that fifty-first rose. That somehow that forgotten flower set the events into motion that led to his death eleven months later on Houston Street.

Ottie squeals over the books I've brought. "Oooh," she says, "I love Travis McGee."

Pearl doesn't look at them. She asks me about my mother. "How's Sara?" she says politely, like her voice might break just saying my mother's name.

"She's giving a poetry reading tonight," I tell my grandmother. Pearl nods stiffly.

"Doris Lessing?" Ottie asks, holding up *The Golden Notebook.* "I don't know her."

"I thought you might like that one," I say to Pearl, but she only nods again, a tight jerking of her chin.

"I've got some great news," I tell her. "I was going to tell you sooner," I add, lying. "But . . . I got into Princeton."

"Princeton!" Ottie shrieks. "A real Harper this one is. Carrying on the tradition. My, my." She beams at me, and her orange lipsticked lips seem to take over her entire face.

Pearl frowns. "I hope you got a scholarship. Surely Sara can't afford—"

"Even with the scholarship I'm short," I blurt out. "Two thousand dollars short."

My grandmother's eyes are milky and blue. They seem to swim lazily in her head, unfocused.

"I'm working like ten jobs," I continue. As if for proof, I show her my date book, a coverless one from the bookstore. I point out how each block of each day is filled with jobs.

She hardly looks at it. Instead, she stands. It is, I know, her signal for me to leave.

"Please," I say, "I'd pay you back."

"If your mother had invested the insurance money, she'd be able to send you."

I sigh. My mother has told me and I have told Pearl that it was my father who cashed in that policy so they could get back to New York from Mexico, which is where they had ended up after meeting on the highway. And with what was left over, he had invested in this florist shop, the one he was delivering flowers for the day the truck hit him. "He was not the type for papers and things," my mother had told me. "The guy he'd invested with just kept the money himself. We never saw it." Pearl never believed any of it, though. Instead, she likes to think my mother took that insurance money and spent it on frivolous things.

We are in the long hallway leading out now. I hesitate.

"Tell her that—" Pearl is saying. "Tell her that if she hadn't spent all the money, you'd be going to Princeton."

A part of me wants to defend my mother to Pearl, to tell her about that old bike and a million other things. But I don't. Instead I point to the door to my father's room.

Very formally, Pearl performs the ritual. The unlocking, the soft announcement of his name. Inside, I see fresh daisies in a bowl and realize that my grandmother must come in here often, to dust and change the flowers. I sit on the bed and run my fingers along the ridges in the corduroy bedspread.

Pearl tells me about his one glorious season playing football at Princeton.

"I know," I say abruptly, standing again.

Above me, on the wall, my father crouches, eternally clutching that helmet, holding that pose.

Tamara and I walk across St. Mark's Place to the Ukrainian church where my mother will read her poetry tonight. Tamara is talking about the fall, college, California. She tells me that she will take karate lessons with her father, stepmother, and little stepsister. That their house has been photographed for magazines. That she will most likely take their old BMW to Berkeley with her.

All I can say is, "I don't want to sit through another bad poetry reading."

"Cheer up already," Tamara sighs.

I walk faster. "Hey!" she calls to me, and when I turn toward her, she is pointing to something in a bin in front of a used-clothing store. She holds up a pair of red-sequined shoes. They look just like Dorothy's ruby slippers in *The Wizard of Oz.*

"Aren't they great?" Tamara says.

I shrug, even though I think they are better than great. They are wonderful. Dazzling. I imagine the magic those shoes could work, hear the sound of the heels clicking together, of wishes coming true. Tamara buys them, just like that, and puts them on right there on the street. Then she wastes more time poking around the other bins while I stand there feeling miserable. Finally she runs to me, her feet a flash of sparkling red.

"Here," she says. "For you." And she holds out a wilted corsage of silk flowers, faded and worn. A peace offering. I want to cry right there on the street. When she pins it on my sweater, they droop sadly. "Divine," she says. "Simply divine."

We get to the poetry reading late. By the time we take our seats—shaky folding chairs lined up crookedly in the basement of the church—a fat lawyer has already started to read his work, poems about hopeless lawsuits concerning malpractice cases and embezzled funds. Tamara looks at me and rolls her eyes wildly. The lawyer has been to our house recently, carrying a briefcase and looking soft and serious.

Then it is my mother's turn. When she starts to read, I slump in my seat. Her poems are always, in some way, about my father and interrupted love. I focus on Tamara's ruby slippers and the way they twinkle.

Now my mother is reading a poem called "The Avalon Ballroom." As a child I imagined it to be a grand place, with twirling lights and soft music, champagne in fluted glasses and romantic couples dancing smoothly across a marble floor. But now I know better. My mother has told me enough times how it was a place where they used to go to hear rock concerts in San Francisco. Still, tonight, my old image comes back to me. The lights there are low, and my father is wearing a tuxedo. He looks like the boy my grandmother loved, a boy with a blond crew cut and clear blue eyes. A boy with a future.

My mother's voice is steady as she recites the poem. She is describing the poster he left us, the psychedelic swirls of orange and mustard yellow, the top-hatted figure with pinwheel eyes. In her poem that figure is my father and the Avalon Ballroom is one more wasted memory.

Afterward my mother invites us to join her and the fat lawyer for Chinese food. I lie and tell her I have to work. "Tropical fish," I say, "over on West Fourth Street. It's a saltwater aquarium, so I have to be extra careful." I don't tell her that her reading was good. But I do tell the fat lawyer. I say, "That malpractice poem was so real." Tamara looks at me like I'm nuts.

"I really think you should join us for dinner," my mother says. She winks at the lawyer.

"Suddenly," I say, "I feel like throwing up."

At home I don't turn on any lights. I don't even open up my bed. I just sit on the couch in the dark. The corsage Tamara pinned on me smells like mildew, but I don't take it off. Somewhere on West Fourth Street there are well-fed tropical fish swimming in perfectly climate-controlled water. I fed them before I met Tamara for the reading, and now I think of them, of their neon colors, their slowly puckering lips. I picture Pearl's milky blue eyes and Tamara's ruby slippers and the elegant false ballroom of my imagination. All of these images swim past in slow motion. I know that tomorrow I will apply to new schools for January acceptance, that those schools will be Hunter and City College, right here in New York, where I won't have to worry about big tuition costs or even room and board.

My mother arrives home in a burst of light, flipping every switch to On and practically blinding me. She lays a feast before me—spring rolls and *moo shu* pork and tiny shrimp in black bean sauce.

"Eat," she says. Her smile is dazzling.

Reluctantly, I pull apart the chopsticks, separating them from each other.

"Please," she says, "let's have a good summer. In September you'll be leaving me and I want beautiful memories."

"Don't worry," I tell her. "I'm not going anywhere."

"Yes, you are," she says.

I sigh. "I've only said it a million times," I tell her. "I don't have enough money to go." I almost add, roughly, Why don't you wake up already? Join the nineties.

"You do," she says softly.

For a minute I think that Pearl must have changed her mind. But then I see the check that my mother is holding out to me.

"The lawyer from tonight," my mother says. "He's an art collector, too."

"So?" I say. The check has my name on it. Lily Harper. It's for twelve hundred dollars. All written in perfect A+ penmanship.

My mother glances at the spot on the wall where my father's poster has hung forever. All that's there is the outline of what used to be there, faint and faded against the rest of the wall.

"It was a collector's item," my mother says, and her voice sounds far away. "Who would have thought?"

I can picture the poster as if it's still hanging there—the swirls, the top-hatted man, the fat blue letters spelling out *Avalon Ballroom* like a boutonniere on his lapel.

My mother keeps on talking about how she read something about these old posters being worth something, how she called first Tamara's mother about it, then Martin.

But I stop listening. Instead, I go over to her and hug

her. She is smaller than me and feels fragile in my arms. She still has on that old blue beret, but strands of silver hair have worked themselves free.

"I think your father would want you to go to Princeton," she says, and her voice is as steady as when she reads her poems. "He'd like that," she adds. "I figure between the two of us we can come up with eight hundred dollars."

"We will," I tell her, not letting go. "We're resourceful."

For a minute, we glide across the floor, gracefully, in a slow waltz. And when we finally separate, the corsage is crushed, and the floor is littered with dozens of old tiny silk petals.

THE CRASH ROOM

David Rice

When my brother Roger and I were growing up, people would ask each of us, "What do you want to be when you grow up?" They weren't asking us if we wanted to be sad or happy or mean or loving; they just wanted to know what kind of work we wanted to do.

It's really a crazy question to ask a five- and six-year-old. But it became a way to compete with each other. To see who could best impress the grownup.

We'd look up at the inquisitive adult and let one of our inner whispers shout out. Roger was quick to shout football player, but he instead became a track star in high school and then later, when he joined the Army, one of the fastest soldiers in his battalion.

I would shout out one of the following with zest: race car driver, jet pilot, astronaut! And at the time I think I meant it, but at the age of eight I saw and touched a dead man. His cool silence killed the blasting engines of cars, planes, and rocket ships. The whisper word was now *doctor.*

My mother was and still is an x-ray technologist, but over twenty-five years ago she was a housekeeper at Knapp Memorial Hospital in Weslaco, Texas. It was the hospital I was born in and the place where Mom cleaned bathrooms and the Radiology department. A woman named Irene told my mother that she could be more than just a housekeeper and taught my mom how to x-ray fingers and toes.

After two years at Knapp, Mom got a job at Edinburg General Hospital decontaminating and sterilizing surgical instruments. The woman who hired my mother and a doctor who saw her potential took it upon themselves to train her to be an x-ray technologist. After six months of training, Mom was on her own and held the job title X-Ray Technologist.

We lived in a town called Edcouch, which was about twelve miles away from Edinburg. The hospital was small, about fifty beds, and did not have a round-the-clock x-ray staff, so the techs took turns taking graveyard call.

Highway 107 between Edcouch and Edinburg had no streetlights and was surrounded by nothing but fields of cabbage, corn, carrots, and cotton. Mom would always take me with her instead of Roger, who shared my father's discomforts. Anytime we had to drop off something for Mom at the hospital, Dad and Roger stayed in the car and sent me in because they would simply get nervous around folks in lab coats.

When Dad went through boot camp, he passed out when they gave him his shots, and Roger couldn't stand the sight of blood. One time we all went to see *Night of the Living Dead* over at a drive-in theater, and neither Dad nor Roger would get out of the car to get some refreshments. They didn't even like going to the cemetery to put flowers on the graves of relatives.

Mom and I, on the other hand, weren't afraid of hospitals or doctors, and I wanted to be a surgeon. I thought that blood was fascinating and that dead bodies were especially cool. And so when Mom was on call, I didn't mind at all losing a couple of hours of sleep.

An ER nurse would phone Mom at odd hours of the night and tell her what kind of x-ray they needed, which determined how fast we had to drive. On those late-night commutes I would be wide awake, driving with Mom, heading toward Edinburg General Hospital. I was Robin next to Batman, speeding in the Batmobile.

I got to see quite a bit and, in the process, I learned medical terminology, the names of bones in the body, and how to develop x-ray film. I would share my hospital stories with my brother, but he wasn't impressed. He would say I was weird or, worse yet, say things like, "I'll bet you look real cute in a white dress." I would chase him, but he was too fast.

When I was fifteen years old, we moved to Austin, and Mom got a job at the Brackenridge Hospital. At the time, it was the only hospital with a trauma center (called the crash room), which also served the city and county. It was a busy place, too busy for me to go and hang around. But soon I was old enough to apply for a job there.

I was seventeen, and the job was to be a patient transporter for the Radiology department. It took a month before I was called in for an interview. In the meantime I worked in a fast food restaurant frying fish.

At school my brother joined the track team and had girls chasing him all over the place. I joined a club for students interested in the medical field and had no girls chasing me. Our sponsor was the school nurse, whom I put down as one of my references, and so I got the job. Of course, having Mom work in the department helped, too.

It was great. I went down with Mom to a hospital uniform supply store and got a couple of white lab coats. When I got home I modeled for the family, but Roger said that I'd probably look better in a dress and laughed. I snapped back, "You wait till you're dying in a hospital and I have to save your neck!" My Mom and Dad got mad and said I shouldn't say such things, but Roger told them not to worry because I'd never be a doctor.

On the first three days of work, Brackenridge put me through an intense orientation, took a photograph for my hospital badge, and trained me in CPR. I thought I looked pretty cool, walking down the hospital halls with my lab coat and badge. I could see myself as Dr. Eduardo Cuellar Aguilar one day. I was the youngest in the department, but I learned fast and worked hard.

Within weeks of working at Brackenridge, I became well acquainted with the x-ray darkroom, memorized the file codes of the x-ray jackets, learned all the departments, knew my way around all nine floors, and knew the names of many of the hospital staff from the housekeepers to the attractive nurses.

I was happy at Brackenridge. The pay was good and I worked only on weekends, which was when all the action came in. I worked twelve to sixteen hours every Saturday and Sunday, and I didn't mind.

X-ray was next to ER, and during the weekends the x-ray staff spent half of their time in there. We had two portable x-ray machines in ER, and both were used every hour. I was a runner between the departments, going back and forth with x-ray film cassettes. I would assist the tech setting up the shot by lifting the patient into position and then standing back with my fifteen-pound lead apron on. A beep would sound out and I would take the cassette back to x-ray, develop the film, and return to ER with another cassette, in case the doctor didn't like the way the film came out.

Portables were done not only in ER but on any floor where the patient was too ill to come down, or if his limbs were surrounded in plaster casts with stainless steel pins sticking out all over the place and cords with weights on the ends, keeping his arms or legs in proper position. Many times these patients looked like human TV antennas or sad string puppets. The Intensive Care and Cardiac Care units had their own portables, and whenever I had the time, I would tag along with a tech to do a portable.

There were always tubes and wires to watch out for when doing portables. Most of the patients would have at least an I.V. going and many had catheters and heart monitors. The floor nurses were sometimes too busy to help the techs with the patient, so my tagging along was appreciated.

There was a small department at Brackenridge made up of kids who just did transporting, but they didn't see as much as I did. They were my age and went to different high schools. Most were the sons and daughters of physicians. When I first met them, they asked if my father or mother was a doctor; they were sort of snobby.

One of them, Jim, was the son of the county medical examiner, and when someone died in ER or on one of the floors, Jim had no problem transporting the body to the hospital morgue, which was in the basement of the old hospital.

Jim and I became good friends, and he would call me whenever he had to transport a body down to the morgue. If his father were there, we could walk around and ask all sorts of questions. Going to the morgue always involved a spooky walk through a couple of long, dim halls, and Jim didn't like to admit that the trip, especially with a dead body by your side, was scary.

There was a way to get there by going through the first floor, but there were usually too many patient visitors walking around, and the dead do deserve respect. Instead we always got into the service elevator and pressed two buttons at the same time to bypass all the floors and get to the base-ment without stopping. The basement was an eerie place filled with machines dotted with red and green lights and huge metal pipes that clung to walls and hung from the ceiling, that snaked their way along and grew more numerous as we guid-ed the corpse through the maze to yet another elevator.

The second elevator was small, with just enough room for the stretcher on one side and me and Jim on the other. We said out loud, "The living on this side, the dead on that side!" We went up one floor, and the door would open to a view of a beautiful, enclosed courtyard, almost a garden. There was a picnic bench in the center, shaded by three big pecan trees standing in a slow breeze and surrounded by lush green Saint Augustine grass. Then down one long cov-ered sidewalk with only half a wall, so you were practically outside, and voilà, the morgue.

It was a small room that smelled of formaldehyde, and in the center of the room was a permanent stainless-steel table. More often than not, there would be a nude body on the table. Illustrations of human anatomy covered the walls, and pens, clipboards, and forms with the seal of Texas were scattered on the two desks of the medical examiners.

When Jim's father was there, he would give a little syn-opsis of their latest case, and sometimes, if he was in the middle of an autopsy, we'd get a quick lesson in anatomy. At the back of the morgue were the stainless-steel refrigerators, no different from the ones in detective movies. They opened like file cabinets, but inside they were cold. We'd pull out one of the empty drawers and lift the body onto the cold metal, sometimes making little jokes as we closed the door. One time we opened the wrong drawer and there was a dead man's body with his right elbow bent, putting his hand in the air. Jim and I pushed the arm down, but it just jerked right back up. We thought it was funny.

The best thing about working at the hospital was that I got to help people. I tried to follow the golden rule. If patients were cold (and you know how cold hospitals are), I would give them a blanket. If they looked real cold or were elderly, they got heated blankets.

It was cool when the doctors in ER asked for me. Since I spoke Spanish, I could translate for them. I would go into ER and talk to the patients and try to make them more comfortable, because being a patient is no fun, especially if you don't understand a word of what is being said all around you. I imagined it must be like being abducted by a UFO.

I was thrilled about surgery and the trauma rooms. Although I never got a chance to watch any surgeries; I did see much in the crash room, where a ballet of lab and x-ray techs, nurses, and doctors took place whenever a patient came in.

In order to be a patient in the crash room, you had to be a Code Three. There were four types of codes. Code One meant you may not feel well, so you'll just have to sit until we get to you, and in the meantime you'll see people who make your petty pain feel silly. Code Two meant that you're probably bleeding and you went ahead of Code One. Code Three was serious, because you are a mess. The crash room was created for folks who may not make it. Code Three was the center of the dance. Code Four meant you were dead. The ambulance drivers would be speeding to Brackenridge with the Code Three patient, and the crash team would be getting ready, but then the drivers would radio in a Code Four and the team would stand down.

But when a Code Three came in, with the patient holding on for dear life, people would be flying in and out of the crash room. Most of the time there would be blood all over the floor, and medical staff left footprints in blood all over ER and down the halls.

Nurses would simply tear away at the packages containing medical equipment and throw the trash on the floor. Everyone had a duty; I.V.'s were started, heart monitors put in place, x-rays were taken, doctors specializing in whatever was the main problem would shout out orders, and people moved—not for the doctors, mind you, but for the patient. It was a rush.

I saw one person die in the crash room and others who died hours or days later. Many times the patient would go straight to surgery from the crash room and the wheels of the stretcher left blood trails. Sometimes I would help lift the patient, and blood would drench the latex gloves that covered my hands. Watching someone else's blood drip down from my fingers to the floor always made me think that somehow it was my blood.

After two years at Brackenridge I began not to like myself. I had become rather insensitive to people's pain and suffering. If I saw someone crying about his minor pains, I would say things like, "Oh, quit your whining." It was an attitude I had picked up from others in the department and throughout the hospital. Especially if they were drunk patients, or were doing stupid things just to show off. Those folks could just sit and wait in the cold hall, and they were lucky if they even got a blanket.

However, this insensitivity was affecting my entire personality. At school I was beginning to have difficulty making friends and keeping girlfriends. Girls I liked said I was callous, and Roger was considered the sweet brother, while I was the jerk brother.

Worse yet, I didn't feel like being a doctor anymore. I didn't see what good all this medicine and medical equipment were doing. Every now and then I would get happy about some patient making a wonderful recovery, but usually it was only because their family members were there every day to support them. The elderly seem to die alone many times. The whole place was depressing me.

I used to visit one man, who reminded me of my grandfather, every Saturday and Sunday. He was there for three weeks, and on the third weekend when I went up to see him, he wasn't in his room. I thought, "Great, he's outta here, he's well." I went to the nurse's station and asked if he had been moved or if he recovered. She looked at me and said rather nonchalantly, "Oh no, honey, he died a few days ago." I tried to look cool, said thanks, and walked down the hall. But once I was in the elevator, I felt weak and was depressed the rest of the day, thinking to myself that I should have paid him a visit during the week.

Now, the only place in the hospital I enjoyed going to was the garden in the old part of the hospital. Just about every time I worked I would go there and sit on the picnic table alone, and eat my lunch, watching the squirrels chase each other.

One day as I sat in the garden I saw Jim wheeling a dead body across the hall toward the morgue. He smiled and waved at me.

"Hey," I said.

He stopped and stood upright from his hunched position, "Guess who this is?"

"Someone dead?" I said with a shrug of my shoulders.

He laughed. "Yeah. It's that guy who was hit by that eighteen-wheeler last week. You know, the guy with the twin baby girls."

I nodded. "What a drag," I said.

"Yeah. Hey, I'll be right out in a minute," Jim said.

I waved back. "Okay."

I looked back across the garden and saw some baby squirrels playing and thought about those baby twins playing alone. Then I looked at the windows of the old hospital where I knew the obstetrics unit was. I realized then that the only way to get out of my depression was to watch a baby being born.

I didn't wait for Jim to come back out. He still thought taking bodies to the morgue was fun, and I didn't care to hear the gruesome details of the man's death.

I wrapped the rest of my sandwich and walked over to the OB unit, and asked the nurses if they would call me to watch a birth. It took about three weeks, but eventually I had the chance to watch a baby take its first breath.

One Sunday morning I was taking a woman who was in the last stages of her labor up to OB. The nurse told me that she would ask the doctor if I could watch the delivery, and he said it was fine with him, but I had only a minute and a half to get into scrubs and mask. I jumped at the chance, dressed fast, and was in the room with my eyes wide open.

The doctor asked the woman, who was in the middle of delivering her baby, if I could assist him. It was crazy. Here was this woman giving birth—she was in real pain, not like those macho men coming in for x-rays of sprained ankles caused by playing tag football or softball—and she lifted her head up slightly and nodded; she couldn't have cared less. I said thank you through my mask. It was an incredible moment for me. A baby boy was born, looking no different from me when I was born. I could hear my heart pumping and I felt as if I could almost see God, as that's how strange yet spiritual the whole thing was.

The rest of the week I was on clouds, but I knew that I had to quit this job. To leave with new blood speeding through me. Two weeks after the birth, I put in my resignation notice. My mother told me that it was a good job, that I should stay, but I didn't feel like watching people die. It seemed to me that no matter what doctors did to save patients, they would eventually die and I didn't want a job like that.

Six years later, my mother was working in a different hospital, and I was dating Marie, who had been an x-ray tech at Brackenridge when I worked there. Marie worked at yet another hospital. Brackenridge was now just a big hospital off Interstate 35, and when I drove by it, I was glad I wasn't there.

But one Christmas season, after I had married Marie, we found ourselves standing in the Brackenridge ER crash room, next to my brother Roger, who lay dying on a stretcher. I was dazed as I stood there. Marie held my hand to give me hope, but we had seen Roger's CAT scan, and he was a mess. He wasn't going anywhere except down to the basement, through the darkness and into the garden.

We knew most of the medical staff, some of whom were even at our wedding, and they all expressed their sorrow. I knew they had done their best because the crash room floor was littered with wrappers and covered in blood. It was a bad auto accident that Roger had been in, leaving him brain dead. Beautiful, smooth brown skin covered his athletic twenty-four-year-old body that now lived only through machines. His soul was ready to fly.

I spoke to him. I told him he was in the crash room. I told him that this was serious stuff, to quit playing around. But Roger never listened to me. He would just walk away with a wave of his hand. But I held his hand tight, wanting him to stay.

His death changed my life. At the wake his friends from the Army and countless of his girlfriends talked about how fast he was. How he ran every day, no matter what the weather. He was training to be the fastest in his division and was a mere second behind the leader. If he could be the fastest, then I could be a doctor.

Medical school wasn't easy for me, but I studied every

day. I imagined I was in a race and that becoming a doctor was crossing the finishing line. When things got hard I pretended Roger was there, urging me on as I did him at his track meets.

I now walk the halls of the hospital with a white lab coat on and stethoscope around my neck and a badge that says Dr. Eduardo Cuellar Aguilar. When I work my shift in ER and hear the ambulance drivers say they have a Code Three coming in, I feel the blood rushing into my legs for a race I always want to win.

TO WALK WITH KINGS

Tracy Marx

Mr. Kirkby, Mr. Kick-Me, Kick-Butt, Kinky—it is the year the new headmaster is no one we like. We *liked* the old one, Mr. Martin, with his wide-open office door and his wife who had no children of her own, so she clutched our warm hands tight in her cool manicured ones. She baked us cookies with jam and chocolate but never smelled of food or the stale heat of a kitchen, only like some kind of flower and the crabapple trees outside her house. To him, we were angels, even after some of us got a "teen" attached to our ages and started getting into trouble—or just looked to people as if we were about to. Then someone decided that Mr. Martin didn't have the right degree, the *proper credentials* for the job he'd had for five years. But what if someone is just good at his job? "These are the rules," said the elders of The Boarding School. "A necessary lesson," as if that were an explanation.

It is the year Claudine Carver's mother takes her home for good, saying nobody is going to turn *her* child into a cook and a cleaner like she has to be. "I didn't rack up a three-

thousand-dollar debt to pay for thirty green acres of suburban grass so that my child would have to cut it," she says,
tossing Claudine's things into the car while the rest of us
look on. We are not used to people leaving. It is, of course,
the new one's fault.

As soon as my best friend Nicky and I see the just-deliv-
ered, ankle-deep carpeting being laid beneath his feet, the jar
of Kraft Caramels gone from the secretary's desk, and the
wide-open office door closed, we know for sure that things
will never be the same.

"Mr. Kirkby comes to us from the Chadwick Military
Academy, with a background in curriculum efficiency planning," announces one of the elders. (They are not all that old,
but their families are.) As soon as we hear the word "military," Nicky swivels her big green eyeballs that look just like
mine sideways at me from under a bouncy, auburn curl of
her hot-rolled hair, and everything makes sense. Scott
Kramer, from our history class, says it's weird how much our
eyes look the same, when all the rest of us is so different. But
I'm flattered because Nicky is already a beauty when it is not
yet clear what I will be. We decide that we are the supernat-
ural descendants of some fantastic, ancient love, perhaps that
of the brave Greek musician Orpheus, son of man and Muse,
for his beloved wife Eurydice. Orpheus journeyed to the
underworld and begged the ruler of Hades to return
Eurydice from death, only to lose her once more in a forbidden glance of his eye. And now their tragic but eternal bond
of love has shown up in our eyes. Mere mortals like Scott
Kramer may be skeptical, but Nicky and I understand the
power of the gods.

"There is a time for change," Mr. Kirkby begins that first
day, sounding so much like he is running for president of the
United States that it isn't hard to suspect he is really talking
about money. It is, according to him, a time for "reallocation

of funds," for "putting our money where our mouths are," for "reaping the glorious fruits of our own labor." But while we are wondering about the labor, the elders are clearly imagining the fruits. Kirkby's clichés only make them drool, with their promise of efficiency and savings—perhaps meaning a new conference room for them, or lunch meetings out. And to the parents, the changes bring the new possibility of a bigger scholarship fund for their kids.

Soon, gone from the cafeteria is Mrs. LaPointe, the chief food server, who through each grade had seen me finally grow tall enough to reach for my own dessert from the highest shelf; gone is Mr. Clifford, who limed the playing fields every spring, drove the snowblower in winter, and raked the leaves in the fall with the help of his crew, who are also mostly gone. And up go the student "work party" assignments: Kitchen Duty, Classrooms, Girls and Boys Dormitories, Outdoor Areas, Gymnasium, Locker Rooms, Lavatories, Infirmary, and many others. Kirkby had found cheaper help. Five of us, from grades six through eleven, are assigned to clean and maintain each area, with one senior in charge of each group. Our groups are to meet at 8:30 sharp every morning, and work for the half hour before the daily Announcements assembly and the beginning of classes. Once a month we'll rotate to a new area. *Some party.* Only the small science building that houses the biology and chemistry labs is excluded, because of all the potentially dangerous chemicals there. Maybe Kirkby is afraid we'll mix up a bomb.

To top it all off, there are the pink slips and green slips, better known as the Kirkby System of Punishment and Reward, made famous during his time at Chadwick Military. That pink and green was the same color combination featured in the local Fancy Pants window display of ladies' golf outfits this year is automatically not a good sign. A pink slip can be given for rule-breaking or misbehaving, like talking back to a teacher or chronic lateness, and a green slip for any extra work or good deeds done, like tutoring another student or baby-sitting a faculty member's child. A certain number of each amounts to either a punishment, like extra clean-up chores or loss of TV privileges, or a reward, like a no-work party day or a special off-campus field trip. In a school where many people both live and work, there are plenty of opportunities to do good—or get caught doing the opposite. Needless to say, pink slips are the easier of the two to come by.

With all his talk of "running a tighter ship," and "getting back on course," I suppose Mr. Kirkby thinks he is going to whip our pampered, private school bottoms into shape, teach us about discipline, cooperation, earning our keep, and all that. "When you are grown," Kirkby assured us, "you'll thank me." What he doesn't understand, or ignores, is that we aren't what we seem to be—a bunch of wealthy, spoiled suburban kids. We're a mixed group—different colors, genders, backgrounds, some from cities, even foreign countries. Most of us understand about money because either our families have it or they don't, and most don't. Some were sent here on scholarships or even borrowed money, because, like Claudine's mother, their families want to protect them from their poverty—even it if means putting up with Kirkby's system, which for many is a small price to pay for rolling hills, tennis lessons, and Latin.

To protect all of us, the parents already voted that we have to wear uniforms so the difference between who is rich, poor, or somewhere in between won't be so easy to see. And for those of us who live at home, as I do, our parents are happy to be spared the drama of our deciding what to wear every day. In our identical pin-stripe skirts and pants, gray blazers, and knee-socks, you could never tell that Claudine's mother scrubbed floors for a living, that Scott Kramer comes from a long line of well-to-do lawyers, or that Nicky's mother, Viv, dances with fire in nightclubs from Las Vegas to Podunk.

Nicky has a newspaper clipping stuck in her mirror that shows Viv with a blazing torch held high just like the Statue of Liberty—except that Viv's leg peeks out from the long slit in her tight, sequined dress, right before she launches into her act. The caption above the photo reads: "A Must-See." When Nicky cries because she misses her mother, because she's homesick for their two rooms in a hotel with no kitchen so they have to wash their dishes in the bathtub, Viv tells her it's her job. "And your job is to be in school, that's *your job,*" she says. Then she sends her the tools of the trade—school supplies, something new to sleep in, to decorate her dorm room with, and even a stuffed animal for company. The morning the package arrives, our homeroom teacher, Mr. Wellington, mistakes the box for some sort of Show and Tell, and encourages Nicky to "share its contents with the class." Confused but obedient, amid the spellbound silence of our classmates, she unpacks the box to reveal a new, pink flannel nightgown, a gingham comforter, a good pillow, and finally, a stuffed purple octopus with huge felt eyes, endless yarn arms, and a name tag that says, "Hug Me, I'm Oscar." The class roars. Mr. Wellington is embarrassed, he apologizes. We never stop telling the story.

Fortunately, our fear that Kirkby's efficiency planning will spiral into something truly serious, like Army regulation crew-cuts, doesn't come true, and it turns out that Nicky and I are mostly assigned to the same work party areas. We don't mind the chores too much: sweeping classrooms, washing down chalkboards, even cleaning the bathrooms—including the urinals in the boy's room that look like long, oddly shaped sinks without faucets. We pinch our noses against the overpowering smell of ammonia as we work. Besides keeping things clean, we also have to be aware of inventory, which means keeping track of the supplies we use, like cleansers, sponges, and paper towels, and helping the senior in charge to know when we are running low so that he or she can make a note on the inventory list.

One of the less unpleasant jobs is to clean the girl's dormitory lounge, which is really like any living room, except that there are two of almost everything, and everything is bigger, taller, grander. Just like at home, we vacuum and dust, but maybe more carefully, lifting the huge rugs, lamps, and vases to make sure we sweep and wipe away the dirt beneath. Just like at home, the TV remote control is always missing, there are magazines strewn across the floor, pennies lost in the overstuffed couches and chairs, and candy wrappers too, even though food is forbidden in the lounge. We use an extra-long-handled feather duster to clean the dangling crystals of the chandelier that hangs from the high ceiling, making it spin and, in the right light, bounce glimmering rays around the room. We need to climb ladders to reach the tops of the arched windows that stretch from floor to ceiling, dressed in layers as if for winter, with linen shades, sheer curtains, valances, and heavy brocade drapes, over the length of which we run the vacuum cleaner hose. Then we spray each pane of glass with cleaner and wipe thoroughly enough to make a squeaking sound with the cloth. There are so many panes that sometimes Nicky and I divide them up like a checkerboard, each of us cleaning every other one.

We do the same when we have to clean the black and white checkered stone floors in the auditorium that was originally a chapel, with its stained glass windows and long pews of connected wicker seats that are so light we can lift and straighten entire rows at once. Some of the floor stones are engraved with the names of people who have been dead for more than a hundred years, and we're not sure whether or not that means they are buried underneath. Sometimes Nicky scares me by hiding in the dank, cobwebby organ room and making ghost noises. Sometimes the dark and quiet of the early morning is eerie.

I can handle most of it, but it is in the kitchen of the school cafeteria that I lose my appetite forever. It is there that I discover the institutional-size tubs of Columbo yogurt that pour a slow slop of strawberry or peach into the two hundred or so never-quite-clean-looking little plastic bowls that land innocently on our trays; oceanic cans of fruit cocktail to feed an army; the smell of salty-sour condiments that permeates the air each time the enormous steel refrigerator or freezer doors are opened and shut—and worst of all, the odious black rubber-lined hole into which leftovers are dumped from trays before they go into the dishwasher. It is in the kitchen of the school cafeteria that I decide some things are better left a mystery.

Standing before the steaming rush of hot water for rinsing the kitchen's huge cooking pots makes me feel as if I'm in a sauna, as if I'm suffocating, the constant sound convinces me I need to pee every five minutes. "Lean into the steam," Nicky tells me, "It's good for the complexion." She says that Veronica Lake, the 1940s movie star she is named after, used to hold her perfect face over pots of boiling water and witch hazel every day. I don't notice Nicky doing the same, however, when it is her turn to scrub.

The kitchen has its good points too, of course. There is kind, funny Mr. Rudolph, the cook, who always jokingly assures me that *he* likes me, "no matter what everyone else says." He teaches me the system for making piles of grilled cheese sandwiches by the hundred: Brush on butter, slap on cheese, stack on next slice of bread, brush on butter, repeat a few hundred times, slap on the grill, wait, flip, repeat. "Hot stuff!" we have to shout when they're done, so that everyone will clear the way while we come through with the full, sizzling pans. Making plain toast is a simpler matter of loading the archaic, oversized toaster, where everything that usually happens on the inside of a toaster happens on the outside, behind wire shelves that turn like a slow Ferris wheel for bread. Then all that's left is to wait and to watch the gradual, mesmerizing rotation of the slices as they transform from soft and white to crisp and golden.

Setting up the self-serve peanut butter and jelly table just before lunch, Nicky and I catch our reflections in the large bowl of quivering, almost black grape jelly. We take care to arrange the various loaves of bread neatly, lining them up from dark to light—pumpernickel, whole wheat, white—even though we know that within seconds of the noon bell, the table will be a ruined chaos of crumbs and discarded crusts, blobs of purple smeared into the pattern of the plastic tablecloth. It's hard not to be discouraged (and when manning the serving station, we have been known to scrape up the occasional gristleburger, cleverly disguised under fresh lettuce and a bun, and dish it out to our most unfavorite teacher). But we try to remember that Mr. Rudolph is counting on us. We're his main help now.

And when Eddie Chase, the senior in charge, wraps his wrestler's arms around me in thanks for a job well done, I think that maybe this work party thing has its moments. "Nothing like having a woman to clean up for ya, huh, Ed?" Nicky says, pulling me just out of his reach. Then they exchange one of those street-smart looks, like a special language people from the same kind of place share. They're both city kids, dipping into this suburban life just temporarily, for school. Nicky doesn't need all this greenery—"cabbage," she calls it, flicking at the bushes and leafy trees of the sprawling campus with dismissive fingers. (But still, I see how she enjoys the scent of freshly mowed grass, the heady aroma of the cherry blossoms when they're in bloom—I catch her holding out her hand to the baby squirrels that seem drawn to her alone.)

For now, though, she is just too cool for this place, even to waste her time complaining about work party. "Just do it," she says, like the Nike sneaker commercial. She has boyfriends at home with names like Ice and Money, which she writes in large, flowing script across the chalkboards, her notebook, inside her desk drawer. She tries to tell me how it feels to kiss a boy. "Just wet your two fingers a little and press them against your lips," she says.

When Nicky doesn't show up for school the first couple of days after a weekend at home, as often happens, I usually imagine that she has run off with a rock star, or spotted Elvis, or been discovered by a Hollywood casting agent. She has already been on the TV show *America's Most Heartwarming Moments,* with her dog Noble, who is her favorite being. Anything can happen in New York, she says. When she doesn't show up, I do her chores. It's an even exchange; I get to copy her math homework.

One morning Mr. Kirkby announces that classes will be suspended on a Friday so that we can all rake and gather the autumn leaves that cover the campus. For this special occasion, we may even wear jeans and sneakers. We greet this news with a mixture of joy and dread. Our joy is at the visions we entertain of digging up handfuls of rich, damp soil and flinging them at each other, of leaping over the creeks that make a dotted line across the fields, of burying each other in aromatic heaps of moist orange and gold foliage. Our dread is at wondering what price we will have to pay for such pleasures.

When Leaf Day comes, it is colder than we expect. The twigs

and pebbles mixed in the hills of leaves we collect are sharp and nick our gloveless hands and fingers as we gather them to stuff into garbage bags. The rake handles feel frozen against our bare palms. Mr. Kirkby, we notice, is wearing gloves, as are his two tiny daughters, their hair the fluffy yellow of baby chicks, following behind him in perfect chick formation. The sight of him marching about, warm and uninjured, surveying our work without doing any himself, does not help his image. I sense Nicky eyeing him, and the rustle of her work quiets. Just as he moves by our corner, she straightens up, turning toward him. "Mr. Kirkby," she calls out, "it doesn't seem to me that we have the *proper credentials* for this type of job." Like in a game of Statues, those of us within earshot freeze, suppressing the nervous laughter that threatens to rise in our throats; the baby chicks are brought to a silent halt by their father, whose usually blank look now registers a sort of pained confusion. On Leaf Day, Nicky gets her first pink slip. We never stop telling the story.

That Friday, for the first time, I go home with Nicky for the weekend. "Pink slip, my patootie!" Viv says when we explain what happened. "I'll show him a pink slip!" she says, lifting her skirt a bit, revealing an edge of lace. Then she lets loose her laugh. She laughs like a hyena, a kookaburra, like Glenda the Good Witch gone mad, like a phone that won't stop ringing, like someone from another planet. She's impossible to imitate. I want to tape-record her and play her for everyone.

"You know what his problem is, don't you?" she says. She's gluing on long, fake nails in Ravenous Red, her granny glasses perched on the tip of her nose. "He's got no grace, I don't care what he's head of. He's haughty. You know, from the French *haut* for 'high, upper'—like uppity." She stops to peer at us from over her half-frames, just to be sure that we

really do know, to be sure *she* isn't wasting her three thousand dollars. (But Viv will pay for the grass. "You don't cut off
your nose to spite your face," she says.) "In other words,"
she continues, "he lacks the common touch. Right, Nick?
What do I always tell you?" Then she rises like a true thes-
pian, her eyes fixed on us, like a hypnotist's, and in a voice I
don't know, she recites:

> *"If you can talk with crowds and keep your virtue,*
> *Or walk with Kings—nor lose the common touch . . .*
> *If all men count with you, but none too much;*
> *If you can fill the unforgiving minute*
> *With sixty seconds' worth of distance run,*
> *Yours is the Earth and everything that's in it,*
> *And—which is more—you'll be a Man, my son!"*

"That's Rudyard Kipling and it goes for daughters, too," she
finishes. Herself the daughter of a showgirl and a disbarred
lawyer, Viv is an interesting combination of press-on nails
and encyclopedic knowledge. And on that note, she goes out
to get us some Chinese food for dinner. "Moo Shu for all my
friends," she declares with a flourish as she exits the room.

"Three drinks for me, don't forget!" Nicky calls after her,
frowning at the mini-fridge in which they have to keep their
food. She wishes they had room for a big refrigerator to fill
with lots of different drinks.

But as soon as she flips on the stereo, Nicky forgets all
about the fridge, the pink slip, and the two tiny rooms in a
dingy hotel. Suddenly it's a disco palace and she's the queen.
Irene Cara is belting out the song "Fame," and Nicky is belting right along. "Fame! I'm gonna live forever, I'm gonna
learn how to fly—high!" She's rapt, leaping from her top
bunk, the windowsill, spinning between rooms, she's everywhere at once, she's larger than life. "I feel it coming together,

people will see me and cry, 'Fame!'" Noble joins in, howling, like her biggest fan.

Nicky believes that Noble, short for Nobleman, is a reincarnated do-gooder, like Robin Hood, sent to survey the city for those in need. Whenever there are more leftovers than will fit in the mini-fridge, Nicky packs them up and Noble carries the bag in his teeth as they go for his walk. They look out for people who are hungry. That was when the *America's Most Heartwarming Moments* crew spotted them. The food is never wasted. There are so many people in the neighborhood who live on the street, who have no jobs at all, maybe because they are sick, or out of luck, or just too sad to work. Viv says that sometimes a person's sadness gets so strong that it becomes a kind of sickness all its own. They are always grateful for the food. Nicky swears that it had to be Noble's idea in the first place, because she is much too selfish to have thought of it by herself.

"I'm gonna make it to Heaven, light up the sky like a flame, I'm gonna live forever, baby remember my name, Fame!" she sings into her mother's face as she comes back in.

"Listen, kiddie," Viv says through the steaming takeout bags, "if you can dream it, you can be it." And our fortune cookies agree.

After dinner, we do our homework. To make it less boring, we read to each other with British accents: "If each member of an equation is multiplied by the same number, the new members will be equal: $2/3x-4x+6$," Nicky reads, sounding Royal Family as can be. But who needs algebra? Nicky is writing a play. When she is working on it, she hangs a string across the room and clips all the pages up with clothespins so she can switch their order around if she wants to.

Later, Viv lets us rummage through her makeup case. We smear on more than our faces have room for, even though the colors aren't quite right. Viv's hair is red, her skin white as can be, while Nicky's is a much warmer peach, like her father's, I suppose. But I don't ask questions. I figure if anyone wants me to know more, they'll tell me.

At bedtime I add to my prayers that the roaches I see crawling on a nearby wall don't crawl on me. I don't say anything, though. What could anyone do? Late into the night it gets cold and Viv lays heavy coats over us while we sleep. The weight of them feels good, safe, holding us in place.

Monday morning, the idea to escape work party comes to Nicky and me at the same time while we're outside, clapping chalk dust from erasers. Maybe the vision of freedom is conjured by the dreamy white clouds formed in front of our faces, or maybe the good weather, or the weekend away; maybe it's the challenge, or just the fact that we've decided not to worry about Kirkby anymore. We know he is not long for the world of our school. We suspect the parents know too, even the ones who believe in chores, elbow grease, noses to the grindstone, and all that. After all, from what we've heard, the scholarship fund hasn't gotten any bigger—only the heads of certain people. Kirkby is really just a visitor living in the big house with the pond and the crabapple trees, sitting at the desk behind the door that was once always open to us. It's too easy to make him look bad, and there is too little to like. He is a youngish man with an older demeanor, bespectacled, pasty-faced, with too little chin to gain our respect, and a suspicious manner. He moves slowly and heavily, as if weights are sewn into the fleshy part hanging from his throat—as if he is stalking the campus in search of our badness. And to our surprise, he seems to find it. But what he doesn't count on is that some will gleefully collect and compare their pink slips—that their approval from each other will be far more important than his disapproval. What he doesn't count on is the grownup hearts budding beneath our buttondown collar shirts and gray blazers. And what else he doesn't count on is what a good hiding place the small science building can be. The next morning, just before the bustle of activity, Nicky and I slip through its heavy doors, with a plan to slip back out just in time for Announcements.

As we walk through the halls while the rest of the campus is busily cleaning, an odd serenity finds us in the empty laboratory environment, with its eyewash-cum-water fountains, the gleaming black Formica of the long, narrow tables, the pungent formaldehyde smell. Set on a hill, the building is a place removed, different from all the other parts of the school, filled with funnels and test tubes, the tinkling of glass and ticking of timers, dripping faucets, and the eerie patter of our lone footsteps. Pausing to look out from our hilltop view, we feel dwarfed by the enormity of the sprawling campus, and for a moment, it doesn't seem so wrong that—under different circumstances, of course—we might want to make some contribution to this, our second home. But then suddenly, just as we are settling into this reflective, leisurely mood, we hear an extra patter, and I feel a flash of heat deep in the pit of my stomach that I recognize as fear. "Kirkby never checks in here," I whisper to Nicky. "Does he?"

"Well, maybe he does today," she says. It strikes me that we haven't thought this scheme through. We're amateurs, but now it's too late. Then Nicky gets an idea. "The ladies room—maybe he won't go in there."

"Right, we can stall him—get it? Stall him?" I say, snickering at my own little pun.

"You're a laugh riot," she says, shoving me toward the door. It's a large room, with six stalls facing a mirrored wall. For a moment we feel safe, until the distant sound of him whistling "Reveille," his favorite tune, draws close.

"Now we're trapped," I say.

"Okay, what about a little acting? We'll say you're 'under

the weather,' like my mother always says when she wants to get out of something." Then she demonstrates, rotating her fingers at her temples and squinting, moaning softly.

"Then we'll have to say it's you instead—you're the one with the talent."

"But you'll probably freeze and go mute." Before I have time to get offended, she says, "Okay, what would Alexander the Great have done?" summoning the aid of her favorite legendary warrior.

"He would not have hid in the ladies room!"

"This is no time for dissent!" she snaps at my panic. But then it doesn't matter anymore, the footsteps are closing in. There's no turning back, Kirkby is definitely coming into the ladies room.

"The stalls!" I say, and we each duck into our own little cubicle. I hear Nicky climb up on the toilet seat so that her feet won't show, while I plaster myself against one side of the metal dividing wall. We hear the door swing open and then his unmistakable, slow steps—not a kingly gait at all, I'm sure Viv would say. I'm hoping that he'll just breeze through and leave. Instead, through the crack in the stall door I see him with his clipboard, counting the bars of soap and hand towels stacked on a nearby wooden shelf, checking off his inventory list. Then, like a drill sergeant without a uniform, he runs his fingers across the length of the wood—a white-glove test without the gloves. Then he stops to wash his hands. After that, he moves to our side of the room.

Step by step, he moves across the row of stalls toward ours, probably the only ones with conspicuously closed doors, and definitely the only ones harboring fugitives. In front of my stall, he pauses. In the stillness, I stare down at his shoes and hope that he isn't staring back at mine. It occurs to me that I haven't situated myself so well, but it's too late to move. And then, it happens, so slowly, but over so fast that it's almost hard to believe. He presses his hand against the stall door, which, in my hurry, I haven't locked. But just as it swings open, past me, and there I am, looking right at him, he turns his head away toward the mirrored wall opposite us. He is looking at himself, and even though I am in his reflection, he doesn't notice me at all. Then he lets go of the door to smooth his hair, and it swings shut again. He doesn't even bother with Nicky's stall. And in the next moment, he's gone. *We never stop telling the story.*

CATSKILL SNOWS

Carolina Hospital

One Christmas holiday, Mother called me at school.

"Viviana, pack your nicest clothes. We'll be there in an hour to pick you up. We're going somewhere special."

"Where, Mom?"

"It's a surprise!"

I had no idea what Mom was up to this time. Through the years I had learned to stop guessing Mother's plans. They were always unexpected and usually didn't take me into account. I was just an incidental in her otherwise impulsive life. After the second war, she married her third husband, Felipe. They made Manhattan their home base and enrolled me at the Hewlett School for Girls in East Islip, Long Island.

Living alone was not new to me since I had also attended a boarding school on the outskirts of Havana. As a matter of fact, I enjoyed it, especially when I was one of the students left behind on the holidays. I would walk the grounds of the old colonial house pretending I was its mistress. In the afternoons, I would get special permission to have tea in the sitting room, with its marble floors and large paintings of aristo-cratic people. On other occasions, I would spend hours in the attic, rummaging through old dressers full of clothes, pho-tographs, and papers as if they belonged to distant relatives. That was the closest I ever got to feeling part of a real family.

Mother and Felipe arrived, three hours later. They walked up the driveway mumbling and giggling—a smash-ing couple, I often heard people say. Even though it was chilly, Felipe wore a white linen double breasted suit and hat; Mother had a striking red wool dress that tightly hugged her hips and then suddenly broke into a cascade of pleats. And of course her red high heel pumps and hat. When they saw me, they stopped their chitchat. Felipe shouted:

"Viviana, how you've grown!"

He kneeled on the steps and kissed my hand.

"You look more beautiful each day," he said as he winked at Mom, "more like your mother."

She jumped in. "Well, we've got to hurry; go get your suitcase!"

"Sure! Here it is. But where are we going?"

"Not yet. We want to surprise you."

As we drove to Manhattan, I thought about Felipe.

Felipe was the bass player for the Lecuona Cuban Boys, a Cuban show band organized by Ernesto Lecuona in 1931. Lecuona took the band to Spain, but after one good season, he became ill and returned to Havana. It was then that Armando Orefiche, the pianist, took over the band. They traveled the world: Cuba, Europe, South America, and final-ly the United States, by train from city to city. Occasionally, I would go with them in the summer and on holidays, like now.

At the train station, we found the rest of the band wait-ing. I looked for my favorite musician, Miguel, a trumpet player, about forty years old. He had joined the band five years earlier after his nightclub in Havana closed down. I had overheard Mom and Felipe talk about his problems with Silvia, his wife. His club had been very successful at first, but after a while Silvia tired of sleeping alone every night. She moved out with their two daughters. He was devastated; he missed the girls. They had always gotten up at dawn to greet him when he returned from the club. Each night, he brought them candy, a flower, a leftover party favor. Anything would make them happy and they in turn would smother him with kisses and hugs. After they moved away, he couldn't stand coming home to an empty house; slowly Miguel began to abandon the club, until finally he lost it.

Felipe found him at a bar late on night and begged him to join the Lecuona Cuban Boys. The trip north, out of Havana and its memories, would do him good.

I knew a lot of this because Miguel often sat by me on the train rides and told me stories about Havana and his girls. One of them would have been around my age; I must have reminded him of her. In turn, I fantasized about his being my father; my own, a doctor, left home when I was four and I never saw him again.

"Hi, Miguel!" I said, stretching up to kiss him. "Where are we going?" I whispered in his ear.

"I'll tell you inside, when we sit down."

When the conductor blew the whistle, I rushed to find a seat next to Miguel. In all, we were about forty: the orchestra, the singer, the dancers, and some of the wives. Felipe had reserved a car exclusively for all of us.

"All right, Miguel, here we are. Tell me!" I said impatiently, tugging at his sleeve.

"We are going to a resort," he said, "in the Catskill Mountains. You've never seen anything like it. It's in the middle of snow-covered peaks and the resort is so beautiful and famous that only the very rich can stay there."

"So why are we going?"

Why? To play, of course! We are the featured band at the New Year's Eve party," said Miguel with pride. "They are calling the party 'Tropical Extravaganza with the Lecuona Cuban Boys.' And important people, rich, classy people from everywhere, will be there. It will be a very important night for us!"

"I'm glad Mami came to get me."

"Sure, honey. We couldn't go without you. How would we rehearse?" he said playfully.

Sometimes I would sing along with the band at the rehearsals. I knew almost every song. Since I was very young, I had a knack for remembering lyrics. I only needed to hear the song once. I never learned to play an instrument, but I loved music and would spend hours in my room singing and dancing.

Some of the musicians unpacked their instruments and began to jam. At fourteen, I was the only child, but I didn't mind; on the contrary, I loved the extra attention.

"Come on, Viviana, sing one for us!" shouted one of the guys. Out of the corner of my eye, I could see Mom's frown and pretended not to notice.

I chose one of those sticky romantic boleros Mother hated. I started with a timid voice, caressing each note. Soon I became absorbed by the lyrics; my heart beat faster and I burst with melodious excitement. I felt defiant and confident. When I sang, I could ignore Mother's reproaches and demands. For a few minutes, I didn't care what she thought.

After I finished, I slowly looked around. Everyone's eyes were fixed on me. Miguel smiled. I became self-conscious and quiet, now back under Mother's spell.

The band followed with a cha-cha rhythm. I was bewitched, captivated by their musical wizardry. The tempo changed from smooth to fast eruptions. I wanted to jump up and let my body answer their call. I didn't dare.

Then there was Roberto. He hadn't been long with the group and was younger than the others. When he smiled, his large white teeth contrasted with his dark complexion. He often smiled at me, but now he was slamming those bongos as if the devil were in him. Drops of sweat ran down his brow; he grimaced with the pain in his fingers. Slowly, everyone stopped playing to hear him. I could hardly contain my exhilaration. When he looked as if he would explode, Felipe broke the spell with a shout.

"Boys, relax! You are going to get exhausted before we even get there."

Roberto looked up, dejected, like a wounded stag. The rest of the guys sighed and put away their instruments. I too was disappointed but glad to have a chance to enjoy the scenery.

"Everyone, look outside!"

The train was entering a totally new world of white splendor. Trees, roads, peaks, all covered by fresh snow.

"Miguel, what are those?"

"Ski lifts, this area is famous for its ski slopes. Most of these towns live from tourists that come up here to ski in the winter."

"It's all so magical, Miguel, as if God had thrown a soft, clean blanket over everything."

Miguel smiled and gave me a quick hug, with a bit of sadness in his look.

I spent the rest of the ride dazzled by the brilliance of the view. I had never seen so much white.

At last, we arrived at the resort. It was bigger and more luxurious than I had imagined. Even our accommodations were impressive. The band members had to stay in a separate wooden building not too far away, immersed in the woods. I ran up the steps to our room, shouting for Mother to hurry.

We had arrived a few days early so the band could plan and rehearse the show on the actual stage. The resort had its own nightclub in the dining room. I was struck by the immense glass chandelier in the middle of the dining hall. To me, it looked like a giant wedding cake with thousands of birthday candles lit around each layer. Sometimes I would come into the dining room just to look at its shimmering lights.

In the mornings, while everyone slept late, I would sneak out of our room and roam in the woods. I enjoyed falling back on the snow, like a feather bed, only a bit colder and wetter, and watching the flurries glide, spotting the branches with white. Then, when I sensed some movement in the main building, I would walk over and watch the elegant people sleepily enter the dining room for breakfast. Even then, I knew I was an outsider, an observer.

In the afternoons, I watched the band rehearse.

About two days after our arrival, the lead singer, Conchita, began to cough incessantly in the middle of rehearsal. She complained of a sore throat and a fever. Armando touched her forehead and confirmed her worst fears. He asked her to return immediately to the room and stay in bed until the day of the show. Mom went for the hotel nurse.

I was secretly happy. As soon as Mother left, I begged Felipe to talk to the band leader; he had let me fill in for Conchita on a few songs in rehearsals. All of a sudden, I had changed from a schoolchild on vacation into Viviana la Rumbera, the greatest singer to leave the shores of Havana. I felt a lot taller than my five feet two inches.

At five feet eight inches, Mom was unusually tall, especially for a Cuban woman, and considered a beauty. I always knew Mom attracted attention with her auburn hair and green eyes. But it wasn't until I was about twelve that

I realized she held a particular allure for males. She took advantage of it too. By fourteen, I knew it was a charm I lacked and I also knew that gave her a sense of relief. I felt the power she possessed only when I was singing, something she could not do.

Surprisingly, that day she went along with my fantasy and let me borrow a costume for the practices. Perhaps she was having too much fun herself, wandering around the resort, pretending she was a guest rather than the bass player's wife. Once, we practiced past midnight until Mom protested and ordered me to bed. I was too excited to care; the band seemed to enjoy my singing. After all, I had a strong voice, danced well, and never complained about the lights being too hot or the dress too tight.

Finally, it was December 31st. We all expected Conchita to be feeling better. The band members got dressed in their white pants with red guaracheras; these were loose shirts with big puffy sleeves trimmed with ruffles in luminescent shades of orange, red, and hot pink, along with matching scarves and waistbands. The women wore similar bright colors on their rumbera dresses, which had long ruffled trains.

I was wearing a special outfit mother had bought me to celebrate New Year's: a sophisticated tight black wool dress that belled out in a gray skirt, accompanied by a red belt and matching red high heel pumps. For the first time ever, she was letting me wear stockings.

We were almost ready for the show when Felipe answered the door. It was Miguel. I couldn't hear what they were saying, but every once in a while they would look over at where I sat on the bed. Felipe would then look at Mom fixing her makeup across the room and shake his head. Miguel kept insisting. Finally, Felipe shrugged his shoulders and let Miguel in.

"Miguel, hi, look at my dress!" I shouted.

"It's beautiful. Listen, honey, I need to speak to your Mom a minute. Can you wait outside?"

"It's all right," said Mom as she continued to comb her hair. "What is it?"

"Armando asked me to speak to you."

"To me? Why?"

"Conchita doesn't think she can do both shows. She feels too weak still."

"That's terrible," Mom said, "but why are you telling me?"

"We think that Viviana could perform instead."

He hadn't finished, but I could see Mom sit up and begin to shake her head.

"Let me finish," said Miguel. "You know how important tonight is for us. We've been rehearsing for weeks, and many influential guests will be there." He hurried on. "We could get other important shows from this one. Viviana could make a difference. She knows all the songs. I'm sure she can do it."

I started to jump out of my seat, but Mother's stern look glued me down. I thought I would lose my heart, that it would jump out of my chest and fly away. But I heard Mom's words.

"No, definitely not. Absolutely not. I won't have it!"

Miguel kept trying, but I knew it was hopeless. I felt sorry for Miguel; he didn't understand that Mother would never give in on this one. I wanted to argue, to shout as Miguel was doing, but I couldn't. I knew Mother would never let me go, and I didn't have the courage to defy her.

"She only has to do the first show, until midnight. Come on," he insisted, "it's New Year's. This would be a great chance for Viviana."

"That's exactly what I don't want, to give her a chance."

"But why not?" asked Felipe.

"Because I want something better for her!" she yelled,

losing her patience. "I don't mind her being dragged around on buses and trains around the country on her holidays, but I don't want that to be all of her life. I want her to have a real home, a normal family."

I could tell those last words had hurt Miguel. With a defeated look, he shrugged, smiled at me, and walked out.

When he left, Mom and Felipe had their first fight. I think after that night, nothing was ever quite the same between them. I sneaked out to avoid their yelling, but I could still hear it from the porch steps where I sat.

"What do you mean, a better life?" screamed Felipe. "How could you talk to Miguel, of all people, like that!"

"Do you call traveling around in a train or a bus half the year a good life?" Mom yelled back. "And having to share an apartment with another couple because we can't afford our own—do you call that a decent life? Well, I don't."

"What do you want?"

"I want something better for her," she answered.

"Just because you put your daughter in fancy boarding schools, it doesn't mean she is better than the rest of us," continued Felipe.

"I never said that!" exclaimed Mother. "I just want her to study. To meet someone who will treat her right, settle down, and give her a normal life."

"A normal life according to whom?" hollered Felipe. "You? Anyway, this should be Viviana's decision to make. She has a beautiful voice, and you know she loves to sing. You may stop her today," continued Felipe, trying hard to contain his anger, "but one day she'll break away for good and then it will be worse, because she'll do it just to get away from you."

"I don't care what you say. I'm telling you no!" answered Mother. "She's my daughter and I will decide what's better for her. I won't have a daughter of mine on that stage. I just will not have it."

At that point, I lost hope of reasoning with Mother. I suppose Felipe did too, because he stormed out of the room, slammed the door, and hardly noticed me as he rushed by.

I ran after him, but I could tell from his rigid walk that he was in no mood to talk. I followed him into the dining hall where the band members were preparing for the show. When Miguel heard me call out his name, he came down.

"What is it, honey? The show is about to begin," he said impatiently.

"I know, Miguel, but I had to talk to you," I answered. "It's very important."

"What is it?"

"Oh, Miguel, I want to sing so badly. I'd do anything! Couldn't you talk to Mother again?" I pleaded.

"I've already tried, Viviana; you heard me. She won't budge," answered Miguel.

"Then let me sing anyway, even if only one song. Talk to Felipe. I don't care what Mother says," I insisted. "I know I can do it, Miguel. I can."

"Of course, Viviana. I know you can do it," said Miguel in a comforting voice, now wrapping his arm around my shoulders. "That's not the point. I can't go against your mother's wishes."

"I don't see why, Miguel. You know she's wrong."

"Now, listen, Viviana," said Miguel. "She has her reasons; one day, you will have yours. Now you must wait."

"Please, Miguel." I started to beg, but the unusually resolute expression on his face stopped me. He was serious. He turned for an instant as one of the band members called to him.

"I have to go now, Viviana," he said. "Go on back to your room with your mother."

"All right, Miguel," I said, gently kissing him on the cheek. "But only because you are asking me to."

He squeezed my arm and turned again.

When I returned to the room, I found Mother calm. The subject was never discussed again. It became another one of our unmentionable topics. We finished getting dressed and went to the dining room where we had places reserved.

From that night, what I always recall most sharply is the band. Neither the fancy clothes of the guests nor the magical chandelier could distract me. In the first set, the orchestra did the best it could without a lead singer and managed rather well. Luckily, the Lecuona Cuban Boys was a versatile group. Each musician played various instruments; Rolando, the sax player, also played the flute and the clarinet. They all danced and even choreographed numbers with the professional rumberos. They put on a real show, with or without a singer.

I sat at the edge of my seat and could hardly contain my enthusiasm. When they began one of my favorites, "Tipi-tipi-tin-tipi-tin-tipi-tipi-tin-tipi-ton . . . el sonido de mi corazon," I knew indeed my heart was beating as loud as those conga drums on the stage. The stage seemed to rise to the skies, and the musicians became my own irreverent gang of angels. The dance floor filled with party favors and hats.

As I looked all around, I could tell I was not the only one swept away by the sounds. The room was transported to a faraway warm place, full of bright greens, yellows, and reds, with exhilarating beats. A place as faraway now as the snow-covered peaks seemed then.

Every once in a while, Miguel would look over at me and wink. I think he felt worse for me than I did. I was too enthralled by the gaiety to feel sorry for myself. However, somehow in the back of my mind I sensed my sadness.

Felipe was right. One day I would have to break away.

That night I couldn't defy Mother or betray Miguel's trust, yet something had changed in me. I realized then that one day I would have to do it; I would have to find my own way, even if it meant disappointing those I loved. I prayed that when that time came, I would find the courage.

The next night, we took the train south again. It was to be my last Christmas abroad for many years. Many holidays have passed since then. I no longer live on Long Island. Yet each Christmas, without exception, I remember that the snow is missing.

DRIVER'S LICENSE

Norman Wong

I was near tears when Mr. Masuda told me that I had flunked my driving test. He accused me of almost getting him killed. Silently, I disagreed with him, but he was the test administrator, a small Japanese-Hawaiian man in his fifties whose skin was wrinkled and darkened by too many hours spent on the golf course, and he had the final say. During the driving test, as we approached an intersection with Keeamoku Street, a wide, three-lane, one-way street, Mr. Masuda instructed me to make a right turn. I turned on my blinker and stopped appropriately at the corner to check for oncoming traffic. As I turned onto Keeamoku, into the right lane, a red Datsun some distance away was coming toward me down the far left lane. Suddenly, the *haole* man in the Datsun switched to the middle lane, and for a moment we rode side by side before he sped by.

"What did you just do?" Mr. Masuda exclaimed. His tiny black eyes bugged. "You almost got us killed."

"No, I didn't," I protested. "He was in the left lane when

I turned. He only switched lanes after the intersection."

"I don't care. You should have let him go by first," Mr. Masuda said, as he frantically scribbled on the test sheet attached to the clipboard.

We returned to the police station. There, my instructor, Mr. Tome, another middle-aged Japanese-Hawaiian man, waited for me. It was Mr. Tome's car that I'd been driving. Mr. Masuda got out of the car and spoke with him.

After a while, Mr. Tome got in. "Sorry about that," he said and suggested I drive the test course again immediately, for practice. "Mr. Masuda said you made a dangerous right turn into traffic. You should always let any cars go by first before turning."

The inside of the white Cadillac smelled tangy-sweet; a perfumed paper Christmas tree hung from the rearview mirror. The interior of the car was done in black leather and felt sticky to me.

"Park here," Mr. Tome instructed.

I attempted to parallel park, going forward and backward and forward again, turning the wheel left, right, left. What was the point anymore?

"What's the matter with you?" Mr. Tome exclaimed. "You did it yesterday."

I had asked Mom to borrow the money for the driving lessons, promising to pay her back as soon as I got a summer job. "What do you need your license at sixteen for?" she'd said. "Where are you going to drive to? With what car?"

"I hope to buy my own car someday," I said meekly. "As soon as I save up some money."

"Maybe you should get a job first."

Then I asked her if she would teach me to drive. She refused. Instead of risking her life in a car with me, she lent me the one hundred dollars for lessons.

Driving home at the conclusion of my final lesson, Mr.

Tome said, "Ask your mother to bring you to retake the test in a couple of weeks. You'll do fine."

I gave Mr. Tome his final twenty-dollar bill.

When I walked into the apartment, Mom was out back on the lanai cleaning the fish tank. Before I could say anything, she guessed. "You didn't get it. Did you? All that money wasted."

I didn't bother to explain to her what had happened.

That summer before the start of my sophomore year in high school, I got a job at McDonald's at Ala Moana Center, where Mom also worked at Jade House Chinese restaurant. Without a license or a car of my own, I caught rides with Mom to and from the mall. After my shift at McDonald's, I would go to Jade House and sit at a back table and wait for Mom to finish working.

Mom and the other waitresses wore Halloween-orange, Oriental-style blouses and black double-knit pants. Nightly, she washed her uniform, disgusted by the smells of cigarettes and grease. Dressing in the morning, she would spray herself fragrant with perfume. I admired most the way that she was able to balance several dishes in her two arms as she walked. I'd never seen her drop anything. She was a big lady, taller than other Chinese women.

When Jade House closed at 10:00 P.M., the waitresses and busboys would come to the back table, where I'd been waiting, and divide up the night's tips. At the large round table, piles of dirty bills were weighed down by quarters, dimes, and nickels. The pennies were cast aside. The bus staff received half-shares, the waitresses full shares of the money.

"Take the pennies," another waitress encouraged me.

"Don't touch them," Mom said to me. "Leave those dirty coins alone."

Soon one of the busboys, who had a short, choppy hair-cut and couldn't speak English, came along and scraped the brown coins into a white take-out box.

"Saving for your future family?" Mom teased the busboy in Chinese. "Who're we going to get to marry you?"

I imagined myself as one of them, a naive busboy recent-ly arrived in Hawaii, working for pennies and thinking, *Someday I'm going to make something out of my life in this new country.*

Sometimes, while I was sitting at the back table watch-ing Mom and the other waitresses divide up the tips, Gary, the manager of Jade House, would come and talk to me. A handsome thirty-something Hong Kongese man (younger and infinitely more American than Dad), he had encouraged me to go to the mainland for college. "It's important for you to be on your own. You can't live at home for the rest of your life. This isn't China." I envisioned myself going to the main-land-United States for college; no one in my family had ever been on the mainland. Gary's thick jet-black hair was slicked back with sweet-smelling grease. He wore designer clothes: slacks, a jacket, a nice shirt opened wide at the collar to show the beginning of a clean, smooth, tanned chest.

"Mr. Playboy," Mom said to Gary, interrupting our con-versation, "where am I going to get the money to send him anywhere? Are you going to pay me more?"

The McDonald's at the mall where I worked was the busiest one in Honolulu. The lines of customers seemed endless. During my first few weeks there I worked exclusively in the front service area. I fried the fries; hot, splattering grease burned my forearms. I manned the soda station, diligently capping the cups as soon as the nozzles stopped running; the last drops of soda turned my hands sticky. In between, I restocked each register with paper bags, napkins, and game pieces; every few mintues, I counted down the sandwiches for the kitchen staff. "Two filets remaining," I warned. At the end of my first month there, I was trained for the cash register.

I was smart in math, so I could count change easily. Even if a worker couldn't, he could still use the register to tell him how much change to give back. But this extra step would slow him down, especially during the lunch-rush's register race; the cashier who brought in the most money from noon to two got a free large sandwich of his choice—any of the Quarter Pounders, Big Mac, or double burgers. When I played, I always won. The other workers, mostly public high school kids, were envious. I went to a private school, because Mom and Dad were Chinese immigrants who valued a good education.

Having quickly mastered the register, I was promoted to the kitchen. I was a failure at frying burgers. The rising, insistent heat of the grill slowed me down. I couldn't keep up with the automatic timer. One day I asked the manager if I could switch stations because the smoking meat was making me nauseated. "What a spoiled, private-school weakling," said the Filipina manager, who had been working at McDonald's all her life. "Go back to the front if you can't take the heat."

I was happiest at the register. It was always entertaining to watch who came in. One afternoon, a young *haole* man, who looked like a tourist, ordered a large Coke from me. He handed me a dollar bill inscribed with a name, Peter, and a phone number, then smiled and said goodbye. Bewildered, I forgot to give him his change.

After my shift ended, I punched out. In the employees' bathroom, I attempted to fix my hair, rumpled by the paper hat that I was forced to wear, and scrubbed the dirty smell of money from my greasy fingers. Later, at home, I would wash my uniform along with Mom's.

Outside McDonald's, I looked around for a familiar face. When I didn't see any, I headed for Jade House.

Sometimes Dad and I had dinner at Jade House. When Mom paid for us she got fifty percent off. Sitting in her section, Mom brought us water, tea, and menus. But before we could even read the menus, she told us what to order. "Order the beef with bitter melon and the shrimp with black bean sauce. They're the only fresh items today. Everything else doesn't look too good."

"So how's school?" Dad asked, pouring us tea.

"Okay."

"What are you studying to become? A doctor? A lawyer?"

"I don't know yet. I'm just studying everything right now." I didn't tell Dad that I wanted to be a writer. Last semester for English class, I had written a couple of stories that the teacher had liked.

"Well," Dad continued, while preparing his soy sauce and mustard mixture in the little sauce dish provided, "the faster you make up your mind, the better off you'll be, and the easier it will be for you down the road. I can't see you as a doctor. With your being sick all the time, you'd probably spend all your time taking care of yourself." He laughed. "But don't take as long as I'm taking to figure out what you want to do with your life." He shook his head.

For almost twenty years, Dad had worked at Uncle's noodle factory. He'd been talking forever about opening a Chinese restaurant of his own. "It's all talk," Mom said. "Open something soon, or soon you'll be opening your own grave." Money was the issue. There never seemed to be enough of it.

I said to Dad, "I want to go to the mainland for college."

"The mainland!" he exclaimed. "Now that would be a

good move. If you go to a good mainland college, when you return to Hawaii you'll have an advantage over all the local kids who only went to U.H. You'll be able to get a better-paying job than the rest of them. But where am I going to find the money to send you to the mainland? It seems like an impossible dream. Unless you get a scholarship. But, of course, you'd have to be really smart."

"I can save up the money I make at McDonald's," I offered.

"You won't make enough there to buy even a one-way plane ticket."

Mom brought out our food—the shrimp, plump and white; the beef, tender and salty; all the vegetables, fresh—Mom was right again. Dad and I ate in silence as we watched her wait on other customers.

She returned with a pitcher of water to refill our glasses. "Before you leave," she said to me, "go and say hello to old lady Wong, the dishwasher in the kitchen. She's always asking about you."

"Do I have to?"

"Yes. It won't kill you."

I headed back to the kitchen. The other waitresses smiled at me as they continued to their tables with plates of steaming hot food. I glanced at the stacks of plates and tea cups lining the shelves, then at the take-out boxes stuffed into each other, white towers rising to the ceiling. Walking into the kitchen I was bombarded by warm smoky air, the sound of clanking woks and metal spatulas, the fragrant smells of ginger, white pepper, scallions, cilantro, and garlic. The cackling cooks, scrawny and dark, imported from Hong Kong, stared at me as I walked by. One said, "That's Chang's son. Look how tall he's grown." A cigarette dangled from his narrow lips. The ashes trembled but never fell as he effortlessly lifted the large metal wok, and with one quick twist of his wrist tossed the cooking food in the air for a split second.

I spotted old lady Wong standing over a large metal sink, washing out a large pot. She turned to me and smiled, showing her gold teeth. Her hair was silver, tied in a bun on top of her head, trapped under a hairnet. She wore a tiny jade Buddha pendant on a solid gold chain. She asked me in Chinese, "Your mother says you're working now?"

"At McDonald's," I told her.

"Good. Good for you to work. Save up your money. Your mother said that you want to buy a car."

"Yes," I said and nodded.

"Save up your money," she repeated. "Without money you can't buy anything." Old lady Wong poured out the soapy water, then began filling the pot again with steaming hot water. The water's violent rush drowned her voice.

For a moment longer, I watched her scrubbing the inside of the pot. She reminded me of my own grandmother, Mom's mom, who had died when I was little. I remembered her lying still in the coffin, her face white with powder. I knew I would never see her again. She used to babysit me when Mom worked. Mom was always working. In an old black-and-white photo, Grandma held baby Mom in her arms. The baby's forehead was wide and shiny. She stared ahead, not smiling. It was hard to imagine the baby was Mom, so vulnerable. Grandma held up her hand to wave to the camera. Who had taken the picture? The grandpa whom I'd never met? What I remembered most about the photo was how poor everything looked. The house in the background was a shack. Paint was peeling off the walls; weeds grew wildly in the yard.

I returned to the table. Standing with a mountain of dishes in her arms, Mom said to Dad and me, "What are you two lazy bums going to do for the rest of the evening while I slave away here? Go to a movie. Go do something together. Don't just go home and lie around the apartment."

I succeeded in getting my license by the end of the summer. Mom repeatedly refused to take me for the test, even after I drove her home from work every night for several weeks. But eventually she gave in. I passed the test with a near-perfect score. After I parallel parked, the test administrator, not Mr. Masuda but a Mr. Sullivan, a kind young *haole* man, took out his ruler, opened his car door, and measured the distance between the car and the curb. "Eight inches. Perfect."

We returned to the police station where I got finger-printed, took a vision test, had my picture taken, and paid the fee. My new temporary license in hand, I stepped up to Mom who sat waiting in the car, and told her to move over from the driver's seat so that I could drive.

"Get funny," she scowled, and refused to budge.

When school started again, I cut back on my hours at McDonald's. Dad suggested that I quit altogether; he didn't want working at McDonald's to interfere with my studying. "It's not worth the pennies they pay you," he said.

But I continued to work weekends and one weeknight because I still wanted a car. As it stood, even with my new license, I still couldn't drive too far on my own. In the evenings I borrowed Mom's car for a few hours when she was at work, but only after promising to pick her up after her dinner shift at 10:30 sharp. Embarrassed, I would excuse myself early from my friends at the video arcade; I couldn't be late picking up Mom.

One Saturday afternoon at McDonald's, my kinder-garten teacher, Mrs. Nelson, stepped up to my register. Even though the last time I'd seen her was ten years ago, I recognized her immediately. I had grown a lot. She had stayed about the same, her hair now white-blonde, her skin wrinkly and tanned.

As she studied the menu, I asked, "Are you Mrs. Nelson?"

"Yes," she replied.

"I was in your kindergarten class," I said.

"Well, you do look familiar," she said, and then glanced at my name tag. "Damon." She ordered an ice cream cone.

I made it extra-large for her. She didn't seem to notice. She was one of my favorite teachers. I had been in love with her. Mom gave me presents—lipsticks and perfumes—to give to her for Christmas and other holidays. I wanted to give her the ice cream cone for free but couldn't, because the Filipina manager was standing in the corner watching me.

"That was my kindergarten teacher," I said to her after Mrs. Nelson left.

"Good for you," she replied sarcastically. "Don't make the cones so big next time."

A few minutes later, she announced, "Register race!"

Automatically, I raced to fulfill my customer's order. First the Big Mac, then the fries nestled beside it in the bag, the top folded over neatly, twice. "That's three fifty-eight, please." The customer gave me $5.00; $1.42 in change, I calculated instantly. Would I ever be able to afford a car of my own? Even with my own car, how far could I go? You could drive around Oahu in less than four hours. I looked out desperately at the long line of customers for a familiar face. No matter how hard I worked, I would still be paid barely above minimum wage. Why was I working so hard?

"May I take your order?" I knew I was good at my job; I served my customers fast and efficiently. I always won register races. But for what? A free large sandwich, whose value was about two dollars?

I looked over at the Filipina manager scrutinizing my performance.

"Faster," she shouted. "Damon, stop staring off into space."

Did I want to be like her when I grew up? Working at McDonald's for the rest of my life, bullying the staff because I wasn't smart enough to do anything else with my life?

I felt myself slowing down. There was no rush. I wouldn't make any more money by wearing myself out.

The only escape was to get off the island, and a car was no good for crossing the water. It was time to move on. I had more important work to do, like figuring out how to get to the mainland. I would have to get a scholarship, but scholarships are awarded only to the smartest people. It was time to quit McDonald's. I had to go home and study.

EGG
BOAT

Nora Dauenhauer

In the fall of every year Qeixwnei and her family went trolling for coho salmon. The season for trolling usually opened mid-summer and the run became intense toward the end of the cannery season when the whole family went to the cannery to earn their money. Her father seined for the canning company while her Aunty Anny and sometimes her mother worked processing the catch from the salmon seiners. Because they worked for the cannery, they lived the summer season in the company houses.

Some years the catch of salmon seiners began to decrease before the seining season came to an end, but around this time coho trolling began to pick up. In order to get in on the favorable runs when the salmon began to migrate to the rivers for spawning, trollers had to be ready.

This was one of the times they were going to go fishing early. Her father had observed on their last trip that there were signs of coho, but he wasn't catching too much salmon in his seine. So he stripped his seine off the boat and began to replace it with trolling gear.

While Pop prepared the gas boat for trolling, the rest of the family packed their belongings from the company houses and transferred them to the boat. Everyone helped get everything aboard.

Mom packed things from their house while Grandma and Aunty packed things from theirs. Qeixwnei and her younger brothers and sisters carried things they could carry easily, and the little ones carried things like pots and pans.

The older boys were big enough to help their father get the boat gassed up and get fresh water for the trip. So they had plenty to do, too, besides helping Grandma and Aunty pack their belongings down to the boat.

When the New Anny was finally ready, they left port in the early afternoon and headed toward Point Adolfus. The tide was going out, and they got on the right current which would carry them fast.

It was on a similar tide the previous year while they were coming to Hoonah from Cape Spencer that Qeixwnei's father spotted a little square-ended rowboat floating on the icy strait. He picked it up and he and the boys put it on the deck of the boat. They had it on deck when they stopped in Hoonah. Everyone saw it and commented on what a nice boat it was. Everyone noticed it wasn't one of the family's rowboats. When they arrived in Juneau, people noticed it too, but no one claimed it. There wasn't a fisherman who didn't know another fisherman or about another's boat, and no one knew whom the boat belonged to.

So Pop brought the boat up on the beach at their home at Marks Trail and started to work on it. He checked the boards to see if they were strong enough to hold the new materials he was going to apply to it and found that indeed they were strong enough and would hold them.

He began to renew it by stripping the old paint off. Then he caulked up the seams and finally put on some green paint left over from some other boat that had been painted before. He put a pair of oars in that didn't quite match. He tied an old piece of manila rope on the bow that could be used to tie it up with.

It was a good-looking boat. It looked just like the flower chalice of a skunk cabbage. And when he tried it, it had balance. It glided across the water very nicely. It was almost as wide as it was long. It was almost round and because it looked like an egg shell, they called it "Egg Boat."

Qeixwnei liked it very much and wanted to try it. She thought the boat was so cute. But when her father told her it was hers, she thought it was the most beautiful boat she had ever seen.

Her own boat! Why, she thought that it was going to be for one of her brothers. She could hardly believe the boat was hers. She was so happy she went around day-dreaming about it for the longest time.

Now she could go fishing on her own boat alongside her brothers, Aunty, and Grandma all by herself. It also meant she might catch a record-breaking salmon that she would fight for so long that she got exhausted from just the thought of it.

Or perhaps she and her Aunty and Grandma would hit a school of fish like she heard some fishing people talk about. She would fill up her little boat, empty it, then go back out and fill it again.

Or perhaps she would catch her first king salmon, and she wouldn't care what size it was just as long as it was a king.

Her rowboat took her through many adventures during her day-dreaming. How exciting the next coho season was going to be. She was so happy.

•

And now they were actually going to the fishing ground. The boat moved along at a good speed. They all worked on their gear, giving it a last-minute check for weak spots and sections that needed replacement.

Mom steered the boat while Pop checked the tackle he would use on the big boat. She ran the boat a lot, taking over completely, especially when Pop had to do work on the deck or started catching a lot of salmon. Sometimes she even engineered. There was no pilot house control, so Pop would ring a bell to signal "slow," "fast," "neutral," "backwater," and so forth.

The boys were playing some kind of a game on deck. They said their gear was ready. Qeixwnei's Aunty wound her line onto her wooden fishing wheel. Grandma was taking a nap. She had been ready for quite some time. She was always ready for things.

As for Qeixwnei, she had her tackle that her Aunty had helped her get together from discarded gear left by various members of the family. She and her Aunty had made a line for her while she was still fishing in her Aunty's rowboat. Her spinner was the one her father had made for her the previous year from a discarded spoon. It was brass metal.

Her herring hook, however, was brand new. It was the one her Aunty had given her for her own. She was ready to fish, completely outfitted with the rubber boots her brother loaned her that were slightly too large.

She was so excited she could hardly eat. The family teased her that she was probably fasting for the record-breaking salmon.

When they finally got near enough to see the fishing ground, there were a lot of power boats trolling and others were anchored. A lot of the hand-trolling fleet was there too. Some of the hand trollers lived in tents out at Point Adolfus for the duration of the summer. When there were no salmon, the fishing people smoked halibut they jigged from the bay over past Point Adolfus. Some of the people were relatives of the family.

When they finally reached the fishing ground, everyone was anxious to get out and fish. They all took turns jumping into their boats while Pop and the two boys held the rowboats for them while the big boat was still moving along.

Grandma went first, then Aunty Anny, then at last Qeixwnei's turn came. The boys followed in the power skiff that was converted from a tender boat for seining.

They immediately began to troll. Grandma and Aunty Anny went close to the kelp beds along the shore line. The boys stayed just on the outside of the kelp while Qeixwnei was all over the place and sometimes dragging the bottom.

She didn't even know where her father, mother, sister, and brothers were. She didn't notice a thing—just that she was going to catch her own salmon. Every time she dragged the bottom she was sure she had a strike.

Evening came and people began to go to their own ports. Grandma and Aunty waited for Qeixwnei for such a long time they thought she wasn't coming in for that night. When they finally got her to come along with them to go back to New Anny, it was near dark and uneasiness came on her. She had completely forgotten all about the kooshdaa qaa stories she had heard, where the Land Otter Man came and took people who were near drowning and kept them captive as one of them. She quickly pulled up her line and came along with her Grandma and Aunty Anny.

Everyone had caught salmon except Qeixwnei. It was so disappointing, especially when her brothers teased her about being skunked by saying, "Where's your big salmon, Qeixwnei?" The rest of the family said she would probably catch one the next day and she shouldn't worry. She slept very little that night. Maybe she never ever was going to catch a salmon at all.

The next day the fish buyer who anchored his scow said that there were fish showing up at Home Shore and that he was going over there to buy fish on his tender.

Pop pulled up the anchor to start off for Home Shore. But halfway between Point Adolfus and Home Shore, the boat started to rock back and forth from a storm that had just started to blow. Chatham Strait was stuffed with dark clouds and rain. So they had to make a run for shelter instead of trolling that day—another disappointment for Qeixwnei, especially after standing on deck most of the way, straining her eyes to see if anyone was catching any salmon.

They holed up all night. She heard her father getting up from time to time during that night. He never slept much on nights of a storm.

Daybreak was beautiful. It was foggy, but through the fog they could see that the sun was going to be very bright. Where the fog started to drop, the water surface was like a mirror except where the "spine of the tide"—the riptide— made ripples of tiny jumping waves on one side and the other side had tiny tide navels. Sounds carried far. They could hear gulls, and a porpoise breathing somewhere, and splashing from fish jumps. It was going to be gorgeous.

They ate quickly and went off to the fishing ground. Once again they took their turns getting into their boats while the big boat moved along.

This day Qeixwnei stuck really close to her Grandma and Aunty. They stayed on the tide spine, circling it as it moved along. She did everything they did. They measured fathoms by the span between their arms from fingertip to fingertip. Qeixwnei also measured her fathoms the same way. She checked her lines for kinks whenever one of them did theirs. She especially stayed close by when Aunty got her first strike of the day. She had hooked onto a lively one. Qeixwnei circled her and got as close as she dared without the salmon tangling their lines.

Then Grandma got her first salmon of the day.

Qeixwnei had just about given up hope of getting a salmon for that day when she got her strike. It was so strong that the strap that held onto the main line almost slipped from her hand. She grabbed for it just in time.

Splash! Out of the water jumped the salmon! At the same time—swish—the salmon took off with her line. The line made a scraping hum on the end of the boat where it was running out.

In the meantime the salmon jumped out into the air and made a gigantic splash. She could hear her Grandma saying, "My little grandchild! It might pull her overboard!" while her Aunty said, "Stay calm, stay calm, my little niece. Don't hold on too tight. Let it go when it runs."

Splash, splash, splash, splash, the salmon jumped with her line. It was going wild. It was a while before she could get it near enough to see that it was a coho and a good-sized one, too. She would get it close to the boat and then it would take off on the run again. Just when she had it close enough to hit with her gaffhook club, it would take off again. Several times she hit the water with the club instead of the fish because it kept wiggling out of range. Each time the salmon changed its direction the little boat did too, and the salmon pulled the little boat in every direction you could think of. The boat was like a little round dish, and the fish would make it spin.

At long last the salmon tired itself out, and when she pulled it to the boat it just sort of floated on top of the water. She clubbed it one good one. It had no fight left.

She dragged it aboard and everyone around her yelled

for joy with her. Grandma and Aunty looked as if they had pulled in the fish. They both said, "Xwei! She's finally got it!" Qeixwnei was sopping wet. Her face was all beaded with water.

It was the only salmon she caught that day, but, by gosh, she brought it in herself. She sold the salmon and with some of the money she got for it she bought a pie for the family. What a feast that was! Everyone made pleasing comments about her so she could overhear them.

They mainly wished she hadn't spent all her money on the pie and that she was going to start saving her fishing money for important things that a girl should have as she grew older.

It was great to be a troller. That fall was a very memorable one for Qeixwnei. Rain or shine she tried to rise with her Grandma and Aunty each dawn.

One day they all timed it just right for the salmon to feed. Everyone made good that day. There wasn't a fisherman who wasn't happy about his or her catch that day. Qeixwnei also made good. When her Aunty and Grandma lined up their salmon on the beach for cleaning, she also had her eight salmon lined up. What a day that was!

When they got to Juneau after the season was over, everyone bought some of the things they'd said they would buy once the season was over. Pop bought some hot dogs for dinner and a watermelon that Grandma called "water berry."

Qeixwnei bought herself a pair of new hip boots. What dandies they were! They had red and white stripes all the way around the sole seams. And they also had patches that read "B. F. Goodrich" on each knee. And they fit perfectly if she wore two pairs of socks.

Her mother told her they were a very fine pair and that they would wear for a long time. Now she wouldn't have to borrow her brothers' boots anymore. In fact, they could borrow hers from time to time. And she could use the boots to play fishing with boats she and her brothers made from driftwood bark at Marks Trail. And very best of all—she would wear her boots when she went with the family to get fish for dryfish camp on their next trip.

DELIVERY IN A WEEK

Thylias Moss

If there was one thing I would have to do, it was work; this was impressed upon me from the beginning of my life when I was in the care of someone who watched me because this was her work, so that my mother could work also, supplementing my father's income so that we could afford to surround ourselves with a few beautiful but unnecessary things that turned out to be the most important objects of our family —paintings of triumph, for instance, that strengthened the wall with watercolor eyes impossible to stare down although these were just a thin layer of paint on canvas; I would look at these faces, one of them a sable princess, whenever I was discouraged. Also ultimately essential were the conch shells so big and substantial my brother and I would fill them with cider and drink it from the narrow tapered end of the conches, and the abalone shells from which we ate our Saturday sandwiches, the pearly rainbow palettes in the shallow bowls seeming to swirl when light hit them.

All day everything I saw was an example of work. Most

beautiful faces were not that way without help; they revealed the efforts of those skilled with cosmetics that existed because there were people dedicated to the manufacture of transforming products as their work. Someone had worked in order to make the book of nursery rhymes that I was able to memorize because my brain worked to establish memory. Someone had worked in order to make the Mott's applesauce that I liked served warm, heated on a stove that hard work, toil in a factory, made possible. The sowing of seeds was the work of wind and gentle hands just as often as it was the dramatic accomplishment of agricultural machines that men and women made, each man, each woman specializing in the making of just one part of these machines. Even audio tapes of lively songs about meadows and streams I'd never seen, except in my working imagination, and the painted renditions of both serious artists and dreaming amateurs were the product of work. The singers' voices themselves were further examples of work, the vocal cords vibrating like harp strings, the diaphragm providing the muscle that amplified the voices; as beautiful and lilting as the singing was, it was nevertheless the result of work. Stuffed animals, electric train sets, softballs, skates—these were created by work, as was the packaged cereal that was effective in appeasing my hunger first thing in the morning. The drawings that were animated into my favorite cartoons were drawn by those who drew for their occupation. And the magician at the state fair did not make magic by accident; the magician practiced and worked hard to create the illusion that no work was involved. Work was continuous and kept track of time as well as a clock, a clock made too by the effort of work. Maybe this is why when the time came for me to take a job, I wasn't distressed; I was used to work, comfortable with work, and couldn't think of anything that work hadn't done. I was dazzled by work. Work was the most amazing idea I knew, especially when something will not succeed unless all its parts work together.

At dinnertime, since our father had died, my brother Blanton said what our father always said while we each stood behind our chairs holding hands before we sat: "We all have a job to do." Then we pulled out our chairs and sat, the steam from hot dishes of food rising like genies, working hard to make even difficult and stubborn wishes come true. Through the steam, sometimes I could see my father's face, just as sometimes while looking into clouds I saw it too, my heart working as hard as it could to pump both blood and life into my memories. Blanton's job was to remind us of what it was like to have masculinity around us, although often masculinity was much like what my mother and I brought to the table; it was full of hope and dreams. But we wanted him to work to make visible to us a strength we thought we couldn't have. Yet he said that he drew the strength that inspired us from us, from the way we urged him to know that he had it within himself.

Years passed and I kept in my mind what Blanton said, the maxim that really many people say, but I took the saying seriously, I always did, because my brother's saying it was a way of keeping something of our father active. *We all have a job to do.* Now if that's taken seriously, the world changes, because you look at it and everything seems busy; everything is or could be involved in making a contribution to the welfare of the world. Clouds have their job bringing rain so that growing won't cease, rivers won't dry into dust, so that thirst won't destroy us; sometimes they roll in just to dim things, tone down the light, make shade, thin the shadows. Clouds have their job though sometimes they perform it with excessive zeal, too much enthusiasm, and then we suffer floods. But maybe, despite their destructiveness, these floods have the job of renewal, turning the land, after the water recedes, into a muddy slate that dries out clean so that rebuilding and revision can occur, Noah's latter-day dove building a nest in the gutter of an abandoned and vandalized house right across the street from the house in which I grew up with Blanton, Mama, and Daddy, building a nest and putting in it eggs from which hatch fledglings that learn to fly away from that decline, their feathers working to empower them, doing the job that has been assigned to feathers, my eyes doing the very important work of seeing this happen, and seeing them leave behind a nest flimsy and uncertain-looking, as if nothing substantial could have come from it, yet that awkward structure had succeeded; it had worked.

I was inspired, so in addition to the hard work I was already doing in school (for which I was paid information instead of cash), I went to work with Gina—anything that could be done together, we did together—washing cars in the local supermarket parking lot on Sunday afternoons when Dean's Food World was closed. We also shoveled snow and, come spring, fertilized and weeded the lawns and gardens of the middle-aged homeowners who were being introduced to arthritis and creaking bones as if castanets were embedded in their legs. I made enough money from these ventures to keep myself in half-way stylish clothes and to afford birthday and holiday gifts, and fresh-cut flowers in winter when my mother became too aware of being lonely. During junior year in high school, I worked on weekends in a movie theater as a cashier in the ticket booth and got my first social security number, paychecks, and bank account, but although people smiled on their way inside the theater and I played a (small) part in their joy by placing in their hands tickets to two hours of escape from their lives, I didn't have the feeling that this job was my contribution to the smooth functioning of living. On the other hand, living was so troublesome sometimes that perhaps it couldn't run smoothly; there was my father's death, for instance, and a month after the junior prom, Gina's family moved away. I decided to try something else.

Telephone soliciting came naturally to me because talking on the phone was one thing at which I had a surplus of experience, considering how Gina and I would nearly burn off our ears from holding the receiver to them for our six continuous hours of conversation every night that proved we were best friends. It's very good too that this job was over the phone where no one could see me (I hope that picture phones never become popular) because I had tried to sell things door-to-door but became very nervous. For one thing, I don't think it's so safe to do that, at least not anymore. And for another thing, because I didn't have the protection of telephone anonymity when I met potential customers at the door, I became all flustered and tongue-tied and quite embarrassed about trying to get them to buy something they probably didn't really need or want, and maybe something they couldn't really afford. All through school, I wasn't good at those door-to-door fund-raising projects—definitely not the job I'm supposed to do! If people need or want something badly enough, they'll attempt to go get it or will arrange for someone to get it for them; they don't sit around waiting for me to bring it to the door coincidentally, if the need is genuine; need doesn't work like that. People don't depend upon accidents to fulfill their needs; accidents and miracles aren't reliable. If it wasn't for how nervous I still become in such situations, I would have considered becoming an Avon lady because I do have an interest in beautifying the planet and making it smell good. Sweetness, you see, too often seems accidental; I'd love to work at making it more deliberate.

I found out about the telephone solicitor job in a classified ad in the newspaper:

BORN WITH THE GIFT OF GAB?

Call 555–6887 and ask for Mr. Ralph.

We're looking for those who are eager to spread the news

by selling the news

in our home delivery special telephone promotion.

IF IT'S NOT IN THE *Franklin Herald,* IT DIDN'T HAPPEN.

It was the word *telephone* that caught my attention; my right hand was practically permanently molded into the ideal shape for holding a receiver. My left index finger had developed a thick pad from speed-punching Gina's number; I didn't even have to look at the number and letter panel when I tapped out Gina's number; I could tell immediately, if the music was wrong, that I had touch-toned the wrong sequence. I had the song to access Gina memorized; sometimes I even hummed it just as I used to study the painting of the sable princess whenever I lost confidence. I knew that I'd get this job, and I was proud to enter the field of journalism where the work was to keep people informed of events and situations that had the ability to affect their lives. Such important work!

Mr. Ralph, when I called, said he liked how my voice sounded over the phone, a trustworthy and friendly voice; he was sure that those I called would want to listen to me, so I was invited to come in for an interview. He said that a resumé would not be necessary. I don't know why I had the idea that I would be the only one interviewing, but when I arrived at the office there were at least fifty others there too, all of whom had been told that their voices sounded like success.

Apparently, we all had the same job to do. I was somewhat skeptical as I took three buses to the address; the office was not located in the *Franklin Herald* building, whose architecture reminded me somewhat of a printing press, but was downtown in a low-rent building that housed apartments above the poorly maintained office for five different small companies. Downtown wasn't thriving as it once was—some sort of gala event every week, glamorous people coming into the heart of city dressed just as ordinary citizens needed for them to be dressed, working hard on their images, impressing even themselves with what they managed to pull off; we who were held back by police with our cameras wouldn't even know that some of our idols had rented the Ferraris and Rolls-Royces and would be incognito when returning the vehicles, using their real names so that no one would be wiser.

Mr. Ralph turned out to be three people, and the offices of these bosses had no walls, just folding partitions between them. Everyone who came for the interview was hired. We had to fill out a simple application and read aloud a paragraph, one of the bosses coaching us to sound more sincere and to read with more feeling and enthusiasm, trying to read the whole passage in a single breath so that whomever we were talking to could not easily interrupt us. I was sixteen years old, the most sincere age of all. The application didn't ask for any references; I didn't think that was an odd omission then, but now I know it was. It didn't seem to matter what, if anything, we'd done before. I just had to fill in my name, date of birth, social security number, date of my (anticipated) graduation from high school, and to answer whether or not I had ever been arrested. Then I had to sign a statement in which I swore that all the information I had listed was correct, but I don't think that any of the Mr. Ralphs tried to verify any information from any of the applications since all who were hired would begin the next day; there wasn't enough time to conduct an investigation. I'd be working for the minimum wage with the possibility of picking up an additional dime an hour if I averaged fifty paid subscriptions a week after four months. There were rows and rows of tables; chairs as close together as seats are at the cinema; a telephone with a shoulder rest for hands-free communication by each chair; pencils, pens, forms, telephone book, and script by each phone. I couldn't believe that the *Franklin Herald,* such a respected newspaper, had facilities like these; I didn't see a single editor or reporter who actually worked in the *Franklin Herald* building; the name *Franklin Herald* appeared nowhere on the premises except in the script.

As it turned out, I actually worked for B & G Enterprises, a company that ran promotions for other companies. All day, I called household after household, going through my list of names in one of ten area communities, highlighting in yellow those numbers where there was no answer; in green numbers where the person I called was hesitant, needed time to think, couldn't say no easily (I'd be calling them again and again if necessary, until they either agreed to subscribe or finally flat-out refused); and putting a bold black X through the names of those who claimed to be subscribers to the *Franklin Herald* already. There was a wire rectangular basket into which I placed completed subscription forms, a red adhesive dot affixed to the upper right-hand corner of the forms for new subscribers who had paid by credit card; the hope was that most new subscribers could be persuaded to pay by credit card, because many who promised to pay by check often did not follow through despite their good intentions. Our telephone books were not the standard residential phone books but modified computer listings that contained even the names and numbers of those with otherwise unpublished phone numbers. Despite such innovations, our lists did not eliminate the phone numbers of subscribers, so many of the calls were unnecessary. Many of the calls were also unwelcome. But the work wasn't difficult and I didn't have to stand on my feet all day experiencing physical drudgery. Although the offices of B & G Enterprises weren't air-conditioned, there were windows that opened out in small rectangles about a foot below the ceiling; once in a while, a bird flew in, once a bat. There was also a loud, powerful fan that afforded us some privacy as we made these calls since the motor tended to drown out the voices of the solicitors next to us.

When I called someone who sounded as pleasant as one of the Mr. Ralphs (one of whom was really a Betty) said I sounded, I was relieved and would sometimes depart from the script to have a regular chat. People like that were too polite for their own good and would listen to the whole spiel even if they were visually impaired and received their news in other ways, perhaps special Braille editions of national papers (the *Franklin Herald* unfortunately had no such edition) delivered free of charge, and of course news programs on radio and descriptive versions on television where someone describes actions and images that dialogue does not explain yet are critical to an understanding of the broadcast; that's what you hear if you press the SAP (Second Audio Program) button on televisions equipped with that feature (for a summer volunteer job, I read books to blind children at a camp, and I recorded books for the local library's Talking Book series).

Most of my co-workers at B & G didn't find telephone soliciting as difficult as I did; most were able to reason that this job was no different from any other. The work was honest; we did not force anyone to subscribe; if the one called said no, then no was accepted; we didn't harass anyone we called and we were to be pleasant and polite, thanking them for their time even if they were rude and slammed down the receivers, trying to damage our eardrums. We had to make a living; some of my co-workers were retired people whose pensions were inadequate. Some were single mothers or fathers who had to support their children and couldn't get a better job. On breaks, we were fond of discussing how we all wanted better jobs, how we all wanted to make a difference if just in our own lives. But many of my co-workers were young, getting our first jobs, the experience that would help us secure the better jobs of our dreams, the real jobs that we were meant to do. I think my father's most rewarding job was his work to make his family understand that we're born to do something worthy and we had to decide what was worth the most, what it would take to fill any empty spaces in our lives; my father wanted Blanton and me to reach beyond selfishness for a job that mattered, and if that job brought to us personal glory, then that was icing, but life was good, could taste good even if wasn't so sweet it could cause a toothache. When it encourages pain, it's too sweet. I wasn't comfortable at B & G.

One woman I called said I sounded so young, about the age of her daughter who had run away; she asked if I could get her daughter's picture in the paper again; it wasn't news anymore, the woman said, since it had been three years since Dora, it was, ran away; she wasn't satisfied with Dora's face on milk cartons, Dora's face on a waxed paper tower, the tallest building on the breakfast table, the one most likely to fire its engines and rocket away into other atmospheres where Dora could no longer be Dora. I couldn't get her to understand that I didn't really work for the *Franklin Herald;* after all, I didn't fully understand that myself. I wasn't as good at this job as I thought I'd be because I listened to Dora's mother and sincerely regretted that I couldn't help. I told her that Dora would probably come back one day. "After you've seen the world," I said, "you realize that home is as good a place as any other; it really doesn't matter where you are, because what you may be trying to escape is everywhere. If it's in the air, you'll always suffer atmosphere, and if it's not, say in space, you're going to take some air with you. So she'll be back, because at home she could breathe. There was no shortage of air even if she didn't like it, even if it wasn't filling or sweet; it did the job of air."

I didn't sell many subscriptions despite assuring those I called that by subscribing now—right now, this very minute, no other—they would receive twenty percent off regular home delivery rates for six weeks if they signed up for a year, and they would become eligible for a drawing for a radio with weather and police bands so that they could be aware of the news as it happened, before it saw that evening's print. "Shall I sign you up for two years? Will you be charging this to Visa or Mastercard? You know, sir, the news is something everyone can use. You can even sign up for a gift subscription for one of your friends or loved ones for an additional ten percent off for six weeks of home delivery; that's thirty percent off the second subscription. Whom shall I send the second subscription to? Delivery will begin in a week."

Even before Mr. Ralph brought it to my attention, I knew that I was selling fewer and fewer subscriptions because I kept calling Dora's mother, at first just to see how she was doing. She was worried about Dora, and I was worried about her. After work, I would go home and think of how empty that woman's life must be without her daughter. My mother had me and she also had Blanton, but this woman had no one. She probably was still holding onto her hope for the work her daughter would do some day. Who doesn't dream for their children? Who doesn't want them to prosper?

I didn't know whether or not she was ever married, but she was alone now. The man in her life at least long enough to become Dora's father was no longer in it. I suspect that her great sadness about Dora was interfering with her ability to date and fall in love again. She probably couldn't try to enjoy herself at all as long as her daughter's status was uncertain. She believed Dora was suffering, and her work as a mother was to suffer with her daughter, to grieve with her and put away levity, leaving it for Dora to find. She didn't say it, but she was so afraid that Dora had been killed, her body discarded and disfigured as if Dora's life had been unimportant. I guess she didn't want to say those words and risk making them come true.

I couldn't get this woman off my mind. Her misery was overwhelming to me yet it wasn't really my misery at all. But if I could be so affected by it, despite the distance from it that I had as a stranger, I realized that this woman had to be helpless to the misery, completely consumed by it. I talked to Dora's mother and talked to her again and again; to Ruth.

Mr. Ralph suggested that perhaps I'd be happier doing some other kind of work, and I agreed with him, so I left. Just like that, I quit my job at B & G. The moment he made his suggestion, I understood immediately what I needed to do in order to be happy and useful. My happiness had become linked to the happiness of Dora's mother. Ruth was so afraid that the media had forgotten about her daughter, that the world didn't care anymore, but I couldn't get Dora off my mind and the plaintive voice of a mother whose desperation was as big as a world. I couldn't pretend that there wasn't work to do for Ruth; I knew better.

Until there's some resolution about Dora, Ruth will not be able to attempt a normal life that, like a roller coaster, struggles to transcend the steep and rugged obstacles, believing that, for that perseverance, there will be the reward of coasting into a valley all dewy with morning and the shadows of hawks, crows, and bobolinks that line the valley floor like fossils proving a better life. And I realized that I cared deeply about Dora and about Dora's mother. I realized that caring was something I did well. In fact, I had gone to B & G because I cared. I could hear Blanton telling me not to waste this caring because it could lead me to my job.

It did. Caring about Dora is my work right now. My conversation with Ruth was a contract that I accepted. And acting on good faith, not reneging on that contract, I will go out into the world and do my caring, recording those books, stocking the local food bank, visiting my elderly neighbor who is the last surviving member of her family, all the time looking for Dora or proof of what happened to her, the key that Ruth can use to unlock life. I'm going to visit Dora's mother, with or without Dora, but I hope hand-in-hand. And if my mother won't mind, I'll give Ruth the certificate I got for organizing the senior project to clean up local playgrounds to hang on the cold wall of Dora's room.

Biographical Notes on the Authors

NORA DAUENHAUER is a teacher and scholar and the author of numerous traditional texts in her native Tlingit language. She has also published poems in many literary journals. She lives in Anchorage, Alaska.

MAGDALENA GÓMEZ is a poet, playwright, journalist, and performance artist. Of the eighteen original theater works she has had produced, the most recent are bilingual plays for children, which tour in repertory with the Enchanted Circle Theater (Holyoke, Massachusetts). She is Theater Artist in Residence at the Holyoke Magnet Middle School for the Arts and has been the recipient of numerous Massachusetts Cultural Council awards for her work as an artist-in-the-schools.

ROY HOFFMAN grew up in Mobile, Alabama. He is an editor, political speechwriter, essayist, teacher, reviewer, and novelist whose reviews and essays have appeared in the *New York Times,* the *Washington Post,* and *Esquire,* among other publications. His novel, *Almost Family,* received the Lillian Smith Award from the Southern Regional Council for the best work of Southern fiction, and the Alabama Library Association Award for fiction. After living in New York City for twenty years, he recently returned to Mobile, where he is Writer-in-Residence at the *Mobile Press Register.*

ANN HOOD is the author of six novels, including the acclaimed *Somewhere Off the Coast of Maine.* She is a contributing editor at *Parenting* magazine and has published short stories, essays, and reviews in *Mademoiselle, Seventeen, Redbook, Glamour,* the *New York Times,* the *Washington Post,* and the *Chicago Tribune,* among other publications. She lives in Providence, Long Island with her husband, son, and daughter.

CAROLINA HOSPITAL is a Cuban American poet, fiction writer, and essayist whose work has appeared in numerous magazines, newspapers, and anthologies. She also lectures on the literature of Latinos in the U.S. She has edited an anthology of Cuban American writers, translated poetry, and has written a book entitled *A Century of Cuban Writers in Florida.*

VÍCTOR MARTÍNEZ has worked as a field laborer, welder, truck driver, fire-fighter, teacher, and office clerk. His poems, short stories, and essays have appeared in many journals and anthologies. In 1996, his novel, *Parrot in the Oven: Mi Vida,* won the National Book Award for Young Adult Fiction. "The Baseball Glove," included in *Working Days,* was originally written as a short story. In a revised form, it became the first chapter of this novel. Martínez lives in San Francisco.

TRACY MARX lives in New York City, where she is a Writer-in-the-College at the Eugene Lang College at the New School for Social Research and works at a New York publishing house. She is also a frequent contributor to *Poets and Writers* magazine. Her autobiographical essay, "Absolutely Someday," appeared in the anthology *Going Where I'm Coming From: Memoirs of American Youth,* also edited by Anne Mazer, and most recently her profile of writer Darcy Frey appeared in *Creative Nonfiction.* The story included in *Working Days* is her first published work of fiction.

ANNE MAZER is a writer of novels, short stories, and picture books for children and young adults, including *Moose Street* (a Booklist Editor's Choice), *The Oxboy* (an ALA Notable Book), *A Sliver of Glass,* and *The Salamander Room* (a Reading Rainbow Feature Selection). She is also the editor of two previous anthologies, *Going Where I'm Coming From* and its fiction companion, *America Street,* both New York Public Library Best Books for Teens. She lives in Ithaca, New York with her son and daughter.

LOIS METZGER grew up in Queens, New York. She is the author of three novels for young adults: *Barry's Sister* (a Parents Magazine Best Book); its sequel, *Ellen's Case;* and *Missing Girls*. Her work has also appeared in the *New York Times, The New Yorker, The Nation, Omni,* and the *North American Review.*. She lives in Greenwich Village with her husband, Tony Hiss, and their son, Jacob.

THYLIAS MOSS teaches at the University of Michigan in Ann Arbor, where she lives with her husband and two young sons. The recipient of many literary prizes, she has published six collections of poetry, including *Rainbow Remnants in Rock Bottom Ghetto Sky* and *Small Congregations;* a picture book for children, *I Want to Be;* and a memoir, *Tale of a Sky-Blue Dress*. She recently received both a Guggenheim Fellowship and a MacArthur Award.

DAVID RICE grew up in Edcouch, Texas, the setting for many of his stories. Though he always wanted to be a writer, he at first studied business and worked as an investigative journalist for his college newspaper. He is the author of *Give the Pig a Chance,* a collection of stories. His short fiction has appeared in several anthologies. He lives in Austin, Texas.

MARILYN SACHS is the author of thirty-four novels for children and young adults including *The Bears' House* (a National Book Award Nominee and a *New York Times* Outstanding Book of the Year), *Fran Ellen's House* (an ALA Notable Book), *The Fat Girl* (an ALA Best Book), *A Pocket Full of Seeds* (a Jane Addams Children's Book Honor Award winner, a *New York Times* Outstanding Book of the Year, and an ALA Notable Book), and *Veronica Ganz* (an ALA Notable Book). She is also co-editor of the highly acclaimed *The Big Book for Peace* (winner of the Jane Addams Children's Book Award and an ALA Notable Book, among other awards). She has two grownup children and three grandchildren, and lives in San Francisco with her husband.

GRAHAM SALISBURY, a descendent of Hawaiian missionaries, grew up on Oahu and Hawaii, and has worked as the skipper of a glass-bottomed boat, a deckhand on a deep-sea fishing boat, a musician and member of a rock band, a schoolteacher, and a writer. He is the author of *Blue Skin of the Sea* (an ALA Best Book for Young Adults and winner of a Parents' Choice Book Award, among other awards), and *Under the Blood Red Sun* (an ALA Best Book for Young Adults and winner of the Scott O'Dell Award for Historical

Fiction, among other awards). In 1992, he won the PEN/Norma Klein award for an emerging voice among American writers of fiction for children and adults.

KIM STAFFORD grew up in Oregon, Iowa, Indiana, California, and Alaska, where he followed his parents as they taught and traveled through the West. He has been director of the Northwest Writing Institute at Lewis and Clark College since 1979, has worked as an oral historian, letterpress printer, photographer, teacher, and visiting writer around the Pacific Northwest, and has taught writing and literature at colleges around the country. He is the author of the picture book *We Got Here Together,* and has published collections of essays, short stories, and poems. His book *Having Everything Right* won a Western States Book Award in 1986. He lives in Portland with his wife and daughter.

NORMAN WONG grew up in Honolulu and now lives in New York City. He graduated from the University of Chicago and received an MA from the Johns Hopkins Writing Seminars. His stories have been published in many journals, and he is the author of the collection *Cultural Revolution.*